The Secrets of Danu

by

Imogene Nix

SECRETS WORLD INTRODUCTION

As the Danu's Secrets trilogy is a continuation of the Blood Secrets & House Secrets trilogies, some readers may come into the series, unknowing of what has gone before. I've added the blurbs for all the Blood Secrets and House Secrets books to assist you to understand the world you are entering. I have also added the blurb for All that Glitters which is a crossover novella between the House Secrets and Danu's Secrets stories.

The Blood Bride Blurb:

Hope just wants to be an ordinary nestling. She went to college and escaped, but now she's back and there's a secret everyone is keeping from her.

Xavier is the new master of the nest, ready to welcome home the daughter of the house who he has never met. He's unprepared for the woman who steals his breath and enchants him.

Now Hope and Xavier must fight for lives and those of the innocents. After all, it is only by overcoming the rogues that they will have a chance of a timeless future together. But will it be in time?

Warning: If you love sexy alpha males that go bump in the night, hot and heavy encounters and strong females, then this book is for you...

The Illuminated Witch Blurb

After years of struggling alone, Celina – a witchling of immense power – must find her place in the world of vampires.

Javed is building a new nest – the first new one in a century – and struggling to overcome his own demons, as an ancient evil stirs.

With Celina in danger, the demands of a fledgling nest and time running out, what are the chances their love can overcome every obstacle?

The Sorcerer's Touch Blurb:

Since the Slaughterhouse Rout, Daniel has nursed his abilities, but the decision he faces will change his life and those of everyone around him.

Whether the change is positive or not remains to be seen.

Cressida fears that history will repeat itself. Once before she lost everything she held dear, but after centuries of hiding she must face her past in order to

forge a new future. Has she waited too long and pushed Daniel away too well?

The darkness draws closer…

Just as the House Secrets book follow the original Blood Secrets series, so do the Danu's Secrets. However, below is a small taste of the House Secrets Trilogy (however Danu's Secret book 1, takes place after House Secrets Book 2.) As Dawn Breaks takes place at the same time as *Blood Secrets* "The Sorcerer's Touch," and is essentially a *continuation* of the Blood Secrets trilogy. To know how the Blood Secrets storyline ends, you do need to read The Sorcerer's Touch.

While the books *can* be read on its own, you have a better understanding of the world by reading the books which precede this one.

In As Dawn Breaks, we finally learn about David and his happy ending.

As Dawn Breaks Blurb:

Genevieve is many things, but no single title fits her quite as accurately as *'mutt'*—the one bestowed by her vicious ex-boyfriend. She's built a life, far from the family who've disowned her—one she's proud of—as a police officer with the Paranormal Liaison Division, and hiding from the world.
David is brittle from his experiences with his ex-wife Alexa, the truth his parents duped him his whole life, and he's trying to come to terms with the fallout of those beliefs, running a nest and feeling like an imposter.
A chance meeting between Genevieve and David opens up an opportunity for hope amid the grim realities of paranormal warfare.
Trusting each other may be their only choice, but the past always bites back and this time is no different.

Edge of Night Blurb:

Pippa is terrified of her step father, Roger—a dangerous and cannibalistic paranormal. For years both Pippa and her twin Peter, have been prisoners, keeping his house and his home in order allowing him to pursue his desires. When Peter has a chance encounter with Simon, they finally have the support to make a run to freedom.
Maxim is a fairy trying to put his life back together, rather than hiding as he's done for the last ten years. Niamh and Simon offer him a home, and a chance to finally achieve his desired career, but chance is a fickle thing, because next door is the timid Pippa and her twin Peter. She innocently ignites his protective side, against his will.
Roger doesn't relinquish what is his easily, and the danger grows

deeper. Pippa and Maxim along with Peter are moved to what should be a safer location, but the danger follows and while their attraction grows, so do the stakes.

House Secrets

How many secrets are hidden from view?

All That Glitters Blurb:

Genny and David had a wild and tumultuous romance, but now the were-pair must travel to Ireland where Genny will undertake her initial education as a leprechaun-were hybrid quickly.

As with all best intentions, things don't go as planned.

Padraic—Genny's father—is placing a wedge between them, and David is spectacularly unhappy with the growing distance between the pair. He just needs her back where she belongs… in his arms.

Genny doesn't see the danger at first, not until the night David doesn't come to her bed, then realisation hits, but with demons and secrets, demanding goddesses and lore all clashing, the two must work together as a couple.

They both know the only way to achieve that is with willpower and love.

The Downfall of Padraic O'Shaunessy Blurb:

Padraic is a leprechaun, long-lived and magical, but even those who have lived for millennia can still be surprised. Meeting Fenella throws him for a loop, because there's just something about her.

Purchasing her family farm isn't just a whim for Padraic—it's the place where he came into the world with his supporters. It's imperative he protects the location of the portal between the hidden world of his past and the human world. Except there's these demons with other plans, particularly Marrer, and it's up to him to stop her.

Fenella is alone and without anyone to help her. Her family is dead, and despite all the hard, backbreaking work she's put into the farm, she's lost it after generations held onto it. There's not much else to do but pack her belongings. That is, until the buyer arrives and asks her to stay.

What is this magic Padraic is claiming she has? Why are dangerous people threatening the property, and why is she so drawn to Padraic? Secrets abound as does danger, and the passion between them is fiery, only there's no certainty they'll survive it.

A Demon Called Grace Blurb:

Running and hiding was Grace's life, but though she was a capable chef and excellent crew member, she had to leave the ship she'd made her home and look for another job. Her plan seems sound, until she's accosted by a man who insists he wants to help her.

Luke's task as a private investigator is to find a woman by someone in a very powerful position. Once he finds here, it's clear Grace calls to him as more than simply his quarry. His inner wolf knows she's special, but the danger surrounding her is deep, and he's determined to keep her safe.

As the darkness continues to grow, so does something else, something *primal*… Once they learn her true identity as a demon, it's not enough to assure his wolf that their combined abilities will ensure their future in dangerous times they have to fight to survive.

The Secrets of Danu Blurb:

Danu might be a Goddess and around since the beginning of time, but that doesn't make her immune… from weariness, from disappointment or from loss.

Berith is a demon, second only to Lucifer and the keeper of the library of hell, but lately something is wrong. Very wrong indeed. His mate is moving against him and building an army to subjugate hell. With all this happening, the pull he feels towards Danu is strangely compelling.

Danu is ready to give up, but one last task lies to her, and it leads to more. It leads to Berith, the one she's loved forever. The one who forgot her. But hope grows in the silence, but will it be enough? Now, she and Berith share hope for a future, if they can only survive the ultimate battle.

Danu's Secrets

Could Danu's secrets overcome the looming danger?

Please note:

The UK and USA share the English language, but there are many words that are spelled differently.

Some words have extra letters in the British spelling, such as the word cancelled. In American English, it is spelled canceled.

There also words that interchange the letters c or s and sometimes z. For example, in America, you spell offense and in Britain, it is written as offence.

We also use the letter u in many words, such as colour and flavour.

These spellings are **not** incorrect.

This book is written in UK English to reflect my Australian/English background.

1

Danu sighed, rubbing the aching pads of her feet. Being a goddess wasn't all it was cracked up to be, especially as less and less people believed in her. That, in and of itself, brought its issues that she'd rather ignore, except it was something she couldn't ignore. The Dagda, father of the pantheon, had warned her that as the growth of other religions entered Ireland, this would be the case. She hadn't believed him at the time. She'd been so full of pride, and now Danu was paying for it.

Of course, she still had all her responsibilities, but also, she had to keep up the act. And that was exhausting.

She brushed her hair from her face and set about preparing dinner. She wasn't a fancy food girl; some might even call her home or cottage style. Unlike other beings, such as Padraic—and she gave a moue at his name—she preferred the quiet of her homestead, hidden in the mists on the island of *Hy-Brasail*. Very few had ever found her private place, and she was well-content with that.

Sitting down at the table, she sighed, looking at the stew cooking on the stove when a breeze swept through. "Aye, Dagda, so you've come again." She rose and turned, her moves slow.

"So I have, girl. Come, we should sit and talk while the tea steeps."

He swept his hand over the table and a pot and two cups appeared. "Her power has grown," he muttered. "Padraic and his wife have found the missing girl. Grace, she's called. She's bringing her man too, a were called Luca. But you must work with the demon to defend what's ours."

Danu knew the day would come. Indeed, she'd known one day she'd need to put aside her façade, but she was weaker now and protecting herself was a necessary first defence. "Dagda, I..." She bit her lip and looked away, the pull of regret and fear overwhelming.

"I know, girl. I too had hoped there'd be more time. Time for you to regain what you've lost. But the time is now, and you must meet with him."

She ducked her head. For too many years, she and Berith had danced around the reality of their situation. She'd kept up the semblance of cold and disinterested, the powerful goddess who was simply above all the plotting and scheming.

"I doubt he'll accept anything from me."

She felt the weight of Dagda's gaze. "Perhaps, but maybe not. His mate has caused him to reconsider a good many things." He poured them each a cup of steaming tea. "I am forever grateful for the man who discovered this brew. Where would we be without it?"

She clasped her freezing fingers around her cup. "I'm also partial to a cup of coffee," she muttered.

Dagda sighed and reclined in his seat. "You were ever a wilful girl."

He'd been telling her that for millennia, sometimes—like now—in jest. Other times, it was with a serious touch of concern. "So, what do you suggest?" she asked.

"I can't tell you how to proceed, you know that, Danu. What I can tell you is that things have been foreseen. Things that lean toward annihilation if you can't put aside your personal differences and work with Berith. I know promises weren't kept, but with your power waning..." Dagda shrugged a shoulder. "You need to find a way to bolster it. To work with him. Because if she..."

"I don't know that I can," Danu whispered. The hurt and sorrow had lodged itself so deeply into her bones that she honestly didn't know if she could forgive or forget.

"If Marrer gets that missing page…" Dagda growled.

She nodded. "I know. I'll… I'll do what I can," she offered, but it gutted her. It was as if she were bleeding and cut to the bone. Just as she'd been then when he'd…

"Good. Good." Dagda patted the hand she'd laid on the table.

She drank her tea in silence, and he seemed to understand she needed time to regroup. Once they'd drained their cups, he flicked a hand, and they were gone. Then he rose.

"I know this is difficult for you," he said. "I regret having to ask it, but…"

"I understand," she muttered, just wanting the Dagda to go. To leave her alone in her solitude.

"You're sure you're fine here?" The Dagda frowned as he reached one last time for her icy hand.

"Aye. It's where I'm best," she answered. And it was true. The quiet curled around her like a loving shawl. It protected and separated her from the hurt and the unforgiving outside world.

"Aye then." And with a nod, he was gone.

She released the pent-up breath inside her, then turned in a slow circle to take in the brick hearth, the simplicity of her surroundings. The house was small and quaint, reminiscent of a cottage of the 1800's, yet it suited her needs perfectly. She'd installed a bathroom, and while that had taken a good pinch of magic, she didn't regret it.

If only she had… *Not that again!*

"A cat might be grand," she considered, but it would need to be fed and watered, and would tie her to a more human timeline of existence. No, she was better on her own. Simpler.

Berith stalked the hallway. Marrer had been pushing back against the wards he'd erected, and he knew that soon, she'd amass enough power once more to attempt to breach his personal space. And into the most carefully guarded area of Lord Lucifer's library.

"You have been in contact with Grace?" He eyed the smaller, lesser demon before him. Grace was the daughter of Vinta, a demon of the library, and one of his greatest supporters.

"I no hear. Grace busy," Vinta said, eyes downcast.

"She's found her mate," he told Vinta gently. In his own mind, he remembered the heady days with Balala. The time they'd spent together. The loving. Then the early days with Marrer. He'd turned to her after Balala's death, needing something… He'd hoped Danu, as his closest friend, might have been there for him. How wrong he'd been.

He hadn't known at the time, but Balala's death had been hastened by his need for a child. One strong enough to take his place at Lord Lucifer's side. It had eventually forced her to go to Danu, seeking power to help her conceive. Danu had given her what she needed, but she'd learned that conception wasn't simply enough. They'd both learned that the hard way.

Danu. What a mess he'd made. His gut burned, but he refused to dwell on the ancient and remote goddess he'd once known as well as himself. The one who'd once been his friend. His confidante.

Where had he gone wrong?

What he'd read in the missive from Balala had brought him up cold. Lord Lucifer had come to see her—a rare honour—but the information he'd shared had brought about Balala's ultimate destruction. Ever since, he'd not laid eyes on his master. It was as if he'd been cast off.

He'd learned much after the binding of Luke and Grace. He'd learned the child of Vinta was part of the puzzle, as was Padraic, the Irish leprechaun who'd taken a half-demon wife in Fenella. He didn't know how, but the couples would be part of their forces against Marrer. His mate. It was predestined.

Marrer. His thoughts returned to his mate. The one he'd turned to in a moment of weakness. When he'd been lost, devastated at the death of Balala and the child.

He remembered now, after they'd become mates, the last time he and Danu had truly been open with each other.

Berith paced, waiting for Danu to arrive. She'd demanded the time, place, and day, so here he was. Once more waiting.

He caught the tingle of her presence and turned.

She held a bottle, wine from long ago. "I thought you could use this. I found a letter for you." She handed it over, and as their fingers brushed, he felt a zing. Fire.

"What is it?"

"Something Balala had me look after." She shrugged. "I don't know what's in it, but I remember the day she came to me. She was only human, after all. Or was, before she became your consort." Derision threaded the words just as it always did when he spoke of her now. Since he'd met Balala, but today it was softened.

He took the paper and broke the seal.

My Lord Berith,
Our Lord Lucifer came today. He told me the offspring will not live.
Cannot live. No matter what I or anyone else does. Its story is already
foretold. The child will be birthed then I, and it, will pass beyond the
shadows.
I do not blame Danu. She did all. Gave all she could and more besides.
She gave me herbs and potions. In the end, she gave me her blood.
Anything to sustain me and the growing babe.
Lucifer tells me that one day a pact will be made. It will weaken all, as
another absorbs the power lost. Just as the power Danu gave me will fail,
so too will Danu falter. She must not fail. She holds the key to all.
Lucifer is going into seclusion. When the time is right, he will come to
you, but until then, you must hold strong against the forces that will rise.
The forces of the underworld. Do not lose hope, for many will be dazzled,
beguiled. It already begins.
It is foretold.

You must be ready. The power already dims in me, my love. But remember, for all time, you hold my soul.

Farewell

Balala

The words rocked him, and he staggered to the seat, slumped down. "How long?" he demanded, shaking the page in his hand.

"Four hundred years," Danu said with a moue of distaste.

"Damn them all," he said, dropping the sheet of paper so he could cradle his head in his hands. "You didn't know?" He lifted his head to spear her with a glance.

Danu shook her head, red hair flying in the still afternoon. "Know what?" She was terrible at lying, having very little guile, he knew from long association. He had to believe her assertion.

He grabbed the page and thrust it at her.

She read, the pink of her cheeks bleeding away, leaving her frigidly pale. "No, that can't be right." Her green eyes sparkled in the sunlight. "This can't be true."

Berith shrugged. "We'll need to find out, because if it is…"

"This changes everything," she breathed.

He still remembered her pallor. The fear in Danu's eyes. Then she'd gone, left him alone, standing in a meadow. He'd called, but she'd ignored him. In time, when she'd come, it had been a coldly remote woman. One who bore little resemblance to the friend he'd lost so long ago. It was the woman he knew now. Berith rubbed his brow and stalked the length of the library.

Marrer raged from her seat, her body a sea of aches as she absorbed the magic from the creatures they'd abducted. "Find the page!" she screamed, spittle flying through the air.

"My lady, we know not its location," said an underling, its leathery, black wings folded hard against its body as it quaked.

"Find it!" she bellowed, and the underling bowed, in deep obeisance, then withdrew through the portal to the chamber beyond.

Marrer's nails, long and sharp, glistened with the scarlet red blood she'd drawn from the other underling, the one cowering on the floor before her. Blood seeping over the rough-hewn floors of her personal domain.

Here, no one questioned her. This was merely a hint of what she was entitled to. What she demanded. Power flowed in her veins, a buzzing wire of heat.

But she needed more. She'd absorb the power from the one before her. It wasn't enough to complete her quest, but for now, it would sustain her lust.

Her fingernails tapped on the arm of her chair. "Soon, I will have enough, and once I have that page, nothing will stop me. Not even Lucifer himself." Her cackle filled the air as she closed her eyes as she remembered the value of the magic. The many things it would accomplish, and the way it tied Berith to her.

2

Danu pushed hard, needing to complete the task before her, the dough stiff and unresponsive. In times past she would have used her powers to create a full larder, but these days, she rationed her power. It wasn't a bottomless well, and she needed enough for her tasks, such as to defeat Marrer. But every day, the spark grew a little dimmer. The power a little less full.

Finally happy, she dropped the dough into a bowl, covered it with a cloth, and set about clearing away the mess.

The tingle she usually associated with a summons was strong, and she sighed. She knew exactly who was summoning her, and she raised her hand. She stood straight, her chestnut-coloured hair perfectly coiled, a sleek, tight curl over her shoulder, and the dress a slenderising bodycon of bronze and scarlet. She didn't have to glance in a mirror to know the perfection of her makeup, the way it highlighted her features. That, she excelled at. After all, this was her armour.

She closed her eyes, folding space and time and stepping forward into the light.

Verdant space shimmered around her. She knew this place well. It was the veiled land of Padraic and Fenella. Turning, she spied Berith waiting on a rock. "You summoned me?" She quirked a brow.

"Indeed," he growled. "We must talk."

She sniffed as the pungent aroma of bovine manure wafted up. "Not here," she stated baldly. Not that the smell was awful. In fact, it was calming, reminding her of the early days, when there were no cities, no bustle, and she'd had hope that someday Berith would understand… She blinked.

Now, she assumed the air she'd perfected over years. "Let's go to the Friendly Bar," she muttered, stalking toward the establishment.

He frowned. "Like this?" He gestured to himself, the tall, dark-skinned creature, with fingers tinged with red, the same as the glow in his eyes. This was his base form, one he rarely assumed, especially if it was somewhere humans might spy him.

"You can disguise it. You know you can. After all, why should I…?" She swallowed the words 'assume a more human form' and instead waved her hands in the air, and he watched.

He sneered. "As you insist."

She hated how remote he sounded, but protection was uppermost in her mind. So she smiled the brittle grin and waited as he assumed the human persona.

"Will this do?" His snarl cut at her. Now he appeared human. Dark hair and fair of skin. His body muscular but just enough. His eyes were chocolate brown and his lips… Soft and framed by a sharp jawline.

"For now," she said and snapped her fingers.

They entered the bar together, and she drifted to the table in the far corner. "I'll have a chardonnay. Cold but not frozen."

He growled and turned to the bar to give the order.

For a moment the steel rod in her spine melted and she was just a girl again. But as he returned, she caught sight of the derision in his eyes. She waited as he slid the glass in front of her.

"You summoned me," she muttered.

"I did. Luke and Grace will arrive in a few days, and I need to talk to you about what you know."

Very little, she wanted to retort, but contained herself. "I'm not sure exactly what kind of information you're seeking."

"Tell me about when Balala came to you."

She quirked a brow. "You know. It was in the letter."

"But why you? Why not Rhiannon or Brigid?"

Danu knew she'd need to explain Balala's reasoning. "Balala came to me, as her family... She was sent by a priestess who told her only I could intercede. They were wrong, and I told them so. I reminded her that Eriu or Rhiannon would be more appropriate, but it seems Lord Lucifer also sent her to me."

"My lord sent her?" He frowned.

"I don't know why, only that he did. Berith..." She blinked, swallowed, but was too slow explaining as Berith rose.

"What are you hiding from me?" His eyes flashed.

"Nothing," she muttered.

"Damn it, Danu. You're... You... *Tuatha De Danaan* hide too many secrets."

She smiled, sorrow filling her. It was the reason they were expelled from heaven—because they knew too much. She'd been young, the youngest of the pantheon to be ousted, but the others, especially the Dagda, had taken her under their wing. She'd been little more than a child, but with a strong grip on her magic, and for that reason, she'd assumed the mantle of the mother of the gods. Not those of the Tuatha, but the others, such as Rhiannon and Cerridwen.

It set her apart.

That's why... *Don't think it.*

"We know much, but we hide much too, Berith. It's our duty. But I cannot help you. I don't know what you seek, only what has been made known to me, and it's not much." She shrugged, sipping her wine, and letting the sharp flavour bolster her flagging spirits.

"You were never this contrary," he muttered, fury a battering chill wind against her fragile defences.

If only he knew just how much those words cut me. "I am a creature of the Tuatha, Berith. But if you have nothing further?" It took every ounce of strength to rise and walk away from him. The fact she didn't shake, nor did her tottering legs betray her, was only because of her pride.

She used it to cloak herself and drew in a little power from it, so that as she stepped away, time and place folded in around herself.

Berith frowned as he watched Danu leave. She'd been curt there at the end. Her eyes pools of green, just like the valley where they'd met. Yes, she'd been perfect in form and figure, but she'd been doing that for years. It wasn't an approach he liked or approved, but he guessed it wasn't up to him.

He wondered, briefly, if she knew how cold and brittle she sounded in the last century or so? If she had any idea that the changes wrought over the centuries had made her seem so remote?

Pushing away the beer, he looked at the humans dotted throughout the bar. What would they say if they knew he was a demon? A creature of the underworld? Or that the woman, the one who'd turned heads as she'd strutted to the table, was a goddess. A woman of immense magic.

His laugh turned to a sputter as a small woman's form, rail thin, with pale blonde hair, entered the establishment. She scurried through the open door. Her head moved back and forth, and his hackles rose when she saw him in the corner of the room. A succubus. What was she here for? Was she meeting someone?

The query was quickly answered, as she slid her way in his direction. "I have a message for you from my mistress." She spoke with a lisp, and he knew it was because she was keeping her identity, the large canines she sported, hidden from the humans. She was a minion of Marrer. A handmaiden, but instead of the weak submissive sort, she was spiteful and vicious—also like her mistress. Fyserlyn was one of the few Marrer trusted, a captain of sorts, who used her power to subdue all the others who were loyal to his ex-partner.

Ex. If only.

"What?" His gaze narrowed.

"We want the page. She demands you hand it over, otherwise she'll take it by force." Fyserlyn didn't pretend that neither of them knew what page Marrer demanded, and he refused to act as if he didn't understand either.

His lip curled. "I don't have it, and even if I did, I feel no compunction about handing it over."

"Then you will regret it." She sniffed the air, eyes rolling up as she decoded whatever it was that wafted on the air. She grinned, a chilling rising of her lips. "I smell something old. Something... A *Tuatha?*" His lips quirked up in a cold facsimile of a smile. "I will be sure to inform my mistress."

On that note, Fyserlyn turned and hurried away.

He swore under his breath. At least Danu could defend herself, couldn't she? After all, she may have lost some of her powers, but she was still formidable. Wasn't she?

He didn't like the path his thoughts were taking, and neither was he comfortable in the form he'd assumed to walk within the world. He did it because he knew anything else could cause too much of a stir.

Rising, Berith approached the door, but he looked over his shoulder one last time, glancing at the bar. Was this the last time? It felt momentous. Then he shook his head and stalked from the establishment.

"Master."

He turned, and a human-shaped demon hovered by the door. But if you looked closely, you'd note the crags on its face and the colour of its skin were just slightly off. And when it opened its mouth, sharp and serrated teeth emerged.

"Padraic called you. Come now?"

Berith snorted. "What does he want?"

"Padraic need plan. Say need to know more."

Berith nodded. He could imagine that was so. And Fenella...well, she basically ran the estate, so he guessed it would be a matter that she needed to know more. How to plan and mitigate any concerns for her livestock. He would, if it was him.

A chill wind blew, and he pulled his jacket just a little closer. "Too cold, topside," he muttered and followed his demon into the small alley between the buildings, so he could fold away through time and space.

3

Danu sighed and filled the basket as she wandered the aisles. At times like this, she wished she could just go back, snap her fingers, and things would occur. That she still had magic to burn. But times and her situation had certainly changed. Instead, she had to deal with the vagaries of a more human life. It wasn't so bad usually, but today the grocers were full of mothers and babies.

It kept reminding her of everything she'd never have. Never experience.

I never had a choice. While some of the Tuatha had taken partners for life, these things had occurred when they were at the height of their powers and before the expulsion. They'd each taken others of similar power, but she'd been far too young, and now?

If only she could wave her hands, make everything better again. If only there were someone for her.

She trudged to the checkout, and paid as soon as her items were packed. Then she headed for the small, quiet area where she usually made her escape, checking to ensure that no one was watching. She stepped into the cubicle when a hand laid on her shoulder. "I need your help, Danu," whispered the tiny demon.

Turning, Danu spied Naamah. "What are you doing here?" she hissed to the small woman.

"I escaped Marrer. She's… killing her servants and absorbing their power." Naamah's eyes were pools of misery. "Along with any others she can take as captive. Marrer butchered my sibling. I had to escape." The pleading in the demon's red eyes had Danu sighing.

"Very well, hold tight and we'll go somewhere safe." But that left only one real location. Her home.

She grabbed onto Naamah's hand, and with a blink they'd entered her home.

"What is this place?" Naamah muttered.

"My home," Danu said, setting down the groceries. "I'll put these away and then…"

"You could magic them," the demon said.

"I could, but this is just as easy." After all, if this was a trap, she didn't want to expose her lack of magic. That would seal her fate.

"So, what Marrer says is true then? Your magic is waning. You're less powerful than you were?"

Danu squinted at the demon, then crossed the room, settling into the seat opposite from the one Naamah had sat down in. "What would Marrer know about my magic?" She carefully hid the hand shaking by folding it into her lap, under the tabletop.

Naamah cleared her throat. "She said you were waning. You'd been too long away from your source and had none other to share." She shrugged.

Danu felt the growth of fear in her chest. If Marrer knew that, what else did she know?

"Tell me everything," she said, waving her arm, so the groceries were in their places, allowing her to settle in.

Berith nursed his tea, glancing out of his home, a grotto he'd prepared millennia ago. With Balala, there had been music and light. Afterward, once Marrer had joined him, it was quiet, but never restful. Full of dark corners and secrets. It was only after she'd left that he was able to regain some skerrick of tranquillity, but it was tainted.

But where else was there for a demon to live? Lord Lucifer had a bolt-hole, hidden from view. Berith wondered, and not for the first time, if he too should consider a magic place. Somewhere hidden and secure.

But now wasn't the time to plan that, was it? Not while Marrer was a threat to humanity.

Most people assumed wrongly that demons were evil. It was true that many were, giving in to base natures. Others, like himself, were more sentinels. Keeping those who should suffer for eternity away from those who served a darker purpose. And of course, hiding all the realities from humans.

"If only it were that easy," he muttered.

Vinta entered the room. "Master, message. Needed quick. Danu sends."

Berith frowned. "What could she want?"

"Marrer," the lesser demon growled.

Without thought, Berith was surging out of the chair. "What has Marrer done? Is Danu in danger?"

"Not know," said Vinta, scrunching up his face.

Something vibrated inside Berith. He had to act but... "Where is she?"

"She send for you. Say follow magic." Vinta looked concerned. "Is safe?"

"I don't know. But I'll go now." Berith clapped his hands to speed his transition. He reeled as he stepped through a doorway. "Danu?"

He glanced across the room, noting that a younger, lesser demon, one he knew as Naamah, sat opposite a white-faced Danu.

"Berith, Naamah informs me your mate knows I'm waning. How would she know this?" Danu spoke through stiff lips, but the mix of fury and terror in her eyes clawed at his insides.

"Waning? I know your magic is less, but waning seems..." He licked his lips. "Isn't that overexaggerating?"

Her lips were white, and she gave a tiny shake of her head. "Not... No. But how would she know? What have you told her?"

"I've told her nothing," he growled.

But there was something at the back of his mind, a half-formed memory that he couldn't quite reach.

"Then how did she know?" Danu demanded, then tossed her head. "Actually, it doesn't matter. What does is that she knows my magic is failing."

The words were a hammer blow. "You can find more." He squinted. "There must be a way."

She laughed, but there was no mirth, only hollowness. "How, Berith? Unlike Marrer, I won't drain others. I won't kill them and steal their magic. The only other ways are through belief. Finding and binding followers to me. I can't do that anymore either."

He stared. "Why not?"

She gulped. "My magic is too depleted. To do that, I must attract them, seed the magic within them. I barely have enough to sustain what I have."

"How... What do you mean?"

"I came here as a youngling. Yes, I was powerful, but for many of my kind, magic grows during the time we are connected to our home. But I'm banished, so all the magic I had? That was all I could count on. I had no one to guide me... Or more accurately, I didn't listen when Dagda tried to school me."

"There must be another way," Berith said, but his senses were quickening, starting to understand her dilemma.

"There is one, as you know. It's joining with another being of magic. One who has either a connection to this place, or..." She licked her lips, and his gaze followed the action. Aware for the first time, that he was seeing the real her. The one he'd not seen in centuries.

"Danu," he prompted.

"The joining allows me to not siphon, but to share the connection, replenish my magic. But they would need to be strong. Someone who is native to this place. Someone as strong or stronger than me." When she smiled, it was crooked. "There aren't many options for me... And unless something happens soon, I'll begin to fade. Eventually, I'll cease to be."

His heart stuttered. "You'll die?"

"In effect, I guess. I'll simply become one with the land. A forgotten footnote in history, and one day, not even that." She rubbed her hand over her forehead. "I've hidden it as best I can, but the truth is becoming more evident every day. I ration my use. I stay here, in my home, and I age." Her lips wobbled.

"So, you must find a mate."

She laughed. "I scared most off, Berith. Didn't you ever notice? I was young during the heydays of belief, and now... Humans don't believe in me or anything except themselves, mostly. The other pantheon members, or those who've survived, are either paired or have committed themselves to a path of oblivion or have begun to find other ways to live. *Human ways.*"

He'd seen that with his own eyes. "Perhaps the vampires or lycans or..."

She laughed. "No. Their magic isn't an empty well either, and while they can replenish, I will not make them suffer my path. To take their magic means there is less for their survival. But Marrer... She must be stopped and..." Danu shrugged, opening her hands. "I'll do what I can, but she is siphoning quicker and quicker. Naamah said she's cutting a swathe through the ranks. Soon, even our combined powers won't be able to stop her."

"Then we must act quickly." But his fear, the one that Danu would cease to be, nibbled at him. "What about Lord Lucifer?"

She blinked. "What about him?"

"Would you..." But as quickly as the thought came, so too did a sense of unease and something else, sly and insidious. It felt... unsettling.

"Partner with Lord Lucifer? I don't think so. I'm not sure he could cope with me, and besides which, hasn't he a harem?" She sighed.

"Harem? No. That's all speculation and untrue. He's not had a partner in a long time, at least a century. Unless something has changed since he entered seclusion. He's particular, it's true." He spoke with conviction, and yet, the thought that Lucifer and Danu… He shook his head, trying to banish the thought.

"No. I'm too set in my ways," she muttered. "Besides, my magic is too low now to attract a suitor. One who can help me, I guess." She blinked. "But what does concern me is if Marrer is growing her power so rapidly, it puts everything else in jeopardy. I…"

She paused, and he waited for her to continue, watching as her eyes dropped to the tabletop.

"I'm not proud of my actions, Berith, but I am still dedicated to protecting my people. I will give everything I have. Everything. But now we need to work together. Put aside our own differences and problems."

His guts churned. *I will give everything I have.* The words weren't lightly given by those who held magic. The words had power, and in that moment, he understood she would stand by them. She would allow herself to wither away, in order to protect those important to her.

Marrer felt the unease in Berith and wondered what could possibly be causing it. Not that it mattered. For many years she'd been draining the connection between Berith and Danu. The one that fortified her magic.

The one neither was aware existed.

"It costs me," she muttered, dropping her blood into the magical well. But it was necessary. After all, if he remembered and knew, nothing would stand between them. "Centuries I've invested into this block. I will not allow it to fall."

She felt the magic and blood sliding from her body. Felt it physically, like a pain.

For a creature such as her, absorbing as much power as she had, it was like a drain was sucking away the energy she held tightly within her.

The magic she'd stolen.

"I need that page," she growled. She'd heard talk about it. Didn't know what it contained, only that it deals with power, obtained through the draining. "I will not be defeated," she snarled.

She dragged her hand away from the opening, watching as the liquid inside spun and whirled ever faster, the colours flashing bright before settling into a dulled gold, purple, and orange. Was it as bright as it had been when she began? Memories were hard to grasp now, as she cradled the hand against her body. The blood dripped down her skin, but she ignored it. Knowing that she'd soon replace what she lost.

"Mistress." Fyserlyn entered the cavern.

"I've told you never to interrupt me in here," she seethed and whirled to see the tiny demon woman who hovered.

"I bring new…" she muttered.

"Begone!" bellowed Marrer, and the creature bowed and withdrew.

This room, it was not a haven so much as the centre of her power. The place where she controlled those who could undo all she'd achieved. "I can't allow that," she said firmly. Not even her brother could enter here.

4

anu considered Berith's suggestion. The conversation picked at the scabs which had grown over her emotional wounds.

Could she change her mindset? Was there hope that she'd yet find a mate? Where would she even begin? It wasn't like gods and magical creatures with sufficient magic were in vast numbers.

She rose, circled the table.

"Danu, perhaps there is hope yet?" Naamah spoke from the corner, and Danu whirled toward her.

"What do you mean?"

"You're not yet depleted. You've a well, one untapped. I can taste it in the air." Her forked tongue flicked out as if tasting something. Her eyes rolled. "Power. So much…" she hissed

Danu's gaze zeroed in on the tiny demon. "Untapped? I have little magic left to me," she muttered.

Naamah shook her head. "I feel the waves, but they are bound. So tight."

Danu gaped at her. "I don't feel that. I feel like I'm nearly empty." She sighed and slumped into the vacant chair. "I know what it feels like to be full. To have magic at the reach of your fingertips. This isn't it."

No, she felt old and heavy. Worn to the bone and without any of the streaks of lightning she had previously associated with a strong dose of magicks.

Naamah stared at her, then shrugged. "I feel. I know. But then, I'm used to Marrer's magic. Oily. Black. Dense."

Staring at the demon, Danu's gaze narrowed. "You speak very well for a lesser demon," she murmured.

Naamah smiled. "I was Marrer's agent, and it was my job to bring humans with magic and others as well to her. To tempt them. There is more to know, but not now," the demon added.

Biting her lip, Danu stared at Naamah. "Is that what you're doing with me?"

"No. You would feel the compulsion. It's one of the reasons I could never do anything with Berith. He knew. He felt. It's like my magic is a grater he said. It wore against his and fed back." She opened her hand and stared at the palm.

Danu shrieked and gripped her head; pain ricocheted throughout it as a ferocious pressure built within her skull. "What?" She couldn't ignore the pain as she stared at Naamah. "What are you doing to me?"

Naamah nodded and the pressure released, but a sharp ache remained. "Grater, that's how Berith described it." She smiled, baring her razor-sharp teeth. "That's what happens when I try to use a compulsion on you."

A moment passed, and Danu had to swallow down the rising burn. "Fine," she muttered, sweating, and nausea rolled in her gut. "Just don't do that to me again."

Berith paced his lounging area, from side to side and back again. "Danu needs to find a mate." The words put him on edge, and he told himself it was only because he wanted to be sure any proposal was suitable.

It didn't mean he liked it. "I don't."

He also refused to question why the thought of it infuriated him. But conversely, he needed to give her hope. Yes, it was in short supply right now, but finding a mate was more palatable than allowing her to fade.

The lump in his chest at that thought was... like a boulder.

They'd been friends once. Close.

He'd known her... Wanted the best for her. *What had changed?*

For the first time, he wondered why there was a blank spot in his memories. What didn't he remember? Because there was something. "Vinta!"

He called for the small demon who came at a run. "You need?"

"What happened between Danu and myself? Why can't I remember why we aren't friends anymore?"

Vinta paled and shook his head, but not before Berith caught sight of his spinning gaze. "No ask me. I not say." Vinta's voice shook.

"What's wrong?" Berith leaned in and sniffed. Vinta reeked of sweat and fear. Terror. "Vinta?"

"I can... no say. Danger," whispered the demon.

"Danger?" Berith repeated the word, feeling like some dumb, ignorant creature, because there was a reason his underling couldn't tell him. It washed off him in waves. Cloying.

"I no... no tell," muttered Vinta, now doubled over and clutching at his guts.

"Vinta?"

"Pain," Vinta whimpered and fell to his knees.

Berith search for a hint as to what was occurring to his faithful friend.

"Tell... danger... death," the demon muttered.

"Then don't, Vinta." He reached out and touched Vinta on the shoulder. "I'll find another way to learn the truth. Just be easy."

Very little upset Berith's equilibrium, but this was taxing him. He felt fear and guilt that somehow he'd caused all this. But what was it he was doing? Was he hiding from the truth? Or was he in some odd way the instigator?

Vinta was still gasping, and Berith frantically searched for some way to ease his friend free of the situation. "I need to find Danu a partner, Vinta. Who would you suggest?"

When Vinta wheezed, Berith frowned. "Are you laughing?"

"Danu not want… partner. She have one," Vinta answered slowly. "I no say, pain bad." Vinta moved sluggishly, levering himself from the floor. "I go. See Grace."

As Berith watched, Vinta dragged himself up and limped through the doorway, and Berith shook his head. "What did I say?" Then he considered what Vinta said. "Danu has a partner?" He frowned. "That can't be. Surely, I'd know, wouldn't I?"

But how would he? The situation between them was strained, and in the past century, they'd only met maybe once or twice in any year. They now were more like friendly enemies.

Danu woke with a start. "At least my head isn't pounding," she muttered.

The sound of creaking from overhead had her frowning until she remembered she'd brought Naamah to her home.

"What was I thinking?" She slid her hand over her eyes. It had been instinctive. She had stepped into the role that came naturally, that of the mother of her people.

She let her hand slide down until it rested on the counterpane. One she'd created long ago, in hopes of…

Tears burned, and she blinked them away. "No time for if's, girl."

She rose and dragged her wrap around herself. A new day had begun, and she had tasks to achieve. Things to do. Plans to make.

Except how could she? After all, she'd made her promise. Pledged herself, so it wasn't like she could really follow through with a promise to anyone else.

The first thing she needed to know was the value of that missing page. What was it, and why was it so important?

She could ask Berith but wasn't yet ready to cope with the physical presence of the demon. After seeing him several times in a short while, it was all becoming a bit much. "And I'm not strong enough to continue to put up the front." This was a truth that denying didn't make better. "Not that any kind of denial works in the long run."

But his visage rose in her mind. True, his demonic form was imposing, with burnished black skin and eyes like wildfires, tall with a musculature most humans could only dream of. His long fingers could be both weapons and the softest touch she'd ever experienced. He was a sight to behold, but he was just as comfortable in human form, and she was well aware, that he was able to balance both with ease.

His human form was equally impressive. She knew that very well. From a chiselled jaw to his chest, he was the ultimate dichotomy. His body was like a velvet-covered tree. Hard and unyielding, strong but protective. His eyes were dark pools, and his lips... "The less I remember that, the better," she muttered.

A new day had dawned, and she had much to attend to. She'd need to meet with Dagda again, see what he knew about the missing page. If he knew more than she did, what it was and where it was hidden.

She headed for the door, but before she reached it, it opened and Naamah stood there, holding a tray. "I thought... Breakfast?"

The tray was covered with a dome, and Danu glanced up to the demon. "You made me breakfast?"

"Yes, I did. I..." She shifted before Danu. "I thank you for your hospitality and care. I..." She dropped her gaze. "I would ask that you take me as your servant."

Danu took the tray and set it on the large bed. "Why?"

"Why?" Naamah blinked at her.

"Why do you want to serve me?" Danu questioned. "Until yesterday, you were in Marrer's service. You swore fealty to her."

Naamah's shoulders slumped. "No, I didn't. My sibling and I were pressed into service by our sire. He owed Marrer for..." She gulped. "It doesn't matter why, but I never swore an oath to her, it's why I was able to leave. Unlike my... sister."

Danu bit her lip. "I want to believe you, but..." She waved her hand.

"Ask my Lord Berith. He will explain, I owe no allegiance to her. I do not answer to her, and she cannot compel me in any way. I am now free."

"Why now?" Danu asked, keeping her voice soft. She needed to know and be sure, and yes, she would check, though maybe not with Berith. Her brain was already spinning around who might be best to ask.

"I stayed for my sibling. She was my twin, which connected us. When she made her oath of fealty, I was stuck. I had no option, because of the call of blood." Naamah sighed. "I... I know most say demons like us cannot bond or be close. Maybe it was the human blood running in our veins, but I loved her, Danu. I stayed to keep her safe, and Marrer knew that."

Many questioned the ability of such spawn to feel deep and innately human emotions, but they'd be wrong. Indeed, many demons were connected, and loved. It was true that though twins in demon spawn were rare, they did exist. It was also true that if one twin made an oath of fealty, it also bound their sibling, so now Danu understood. Blood was the single defining factor in these oaths. She'd seen, often enough, the way demons allowed themselves to bleed to complete the binding to masters.

"Let's allow ourselves some time to see if we can work together," Danu said.

Naamah paled. "While I'm unattached, I'm at risk. You taking me as your servant, I'd be under your protection."

Danu bit her lip. "I... I don't have the power to protect you, Naamah."

The demon sighed. "You don't need power, just to accept me."

"But I..."

"Please, Lady Danu. I need your help. You allowing me servitude with you means I can be safe from Marrer's clutches. Besides, perhaps that will allow you to gain more magic. I am capable of assisting you to gain followers."

"I don't need someone compelled to believe in me," Danu retorted, the thought of it repugnant.

"No, I'm not suggesting I compel anyone. But by spreading the word, sharing what you've done for others, how you've helped..." Naamah shrugged, and Danu had to admit to herself that new believers would certainly assist with her dwindling power supply.

"I need time," Danu said weakly, because she knew there was truth in what the demon was saying. "I..."

The demon stared at her, and she realised this was a gift. One that couldn't be given lightly. Oaths were binding...

"Alright then," Danu said. "But I will not expect nor accept a blood offering, Naamah."

"Thank you, Lady. I will serve you with honesty and integrity."

Naamah reached for Danu's hand, and the frisson of power, the acceptance of fealty, was a jolt to her. She'd forgotten just how strong the punch of power could be.

5

Berith glanced down the rows of books. Books of power, books of knowledge. Books of predestination. Thousands of similarly bound tomes which he'd curated for millennia.

Set on the large reading table at the end of the main room was the book. The one with the missing page. The one Marrer demanded. What was it about that particular title which was the focus of such power?

He marched down, settled himself into the deep chair, and sighed, opening the cover. The pages were old, crisply brittle, and smelled of the must associated with age. The pages were foxed, with blotches and brown spots and spidery lines. The illuminated script was decorated in striking gold, bright azurite, vermillion, and burnt umber among other colours. Similar to monasteries, the underworld too had kept records of a highly ornate nature.

His hands skimmed the lines, as Berith remembered vaguely many of the books he too had assisted in creating. He read the information, considering the message. This book spoke about Lucifer's descent to the underworld. It explained in detail his role and responsibility and why this fall had taken place.

It also named Lucifer's most trusted seconds, designating Berith as librarian and effective second. "A great honour it is to serve my lord."

Berith was proud of what he'd achieved, but since Lucifer's seclusion, things had devolved. Lucifer's assistant had ceased to marshal the troops to protect the underworld, and this had allowed Marrer's rise.

In fact, he'd not seen Lucifuge Rofocale in some time. His mind turned to the chaos now reigning. Smaller cliques had formed, but it was Marrer and her brother, Zazrael, as her subordinate, who had formed the strongest group. They'd been slowly absorbing the lesser forces. Without Lucifuge to enact the rules of Lucifer and to keep the peace, things were becoming far more volatile.

Berith turned the page and smiled. Here lay the truth behind the eviction of Lucifer, that it wasn't so much that he was fallen, as was ordered to take up the role. He hadn't liked it but had nonetheless complied.

The next pages talked about the roles of the varied sergeants, and the importance of keeping the library. This was his head of power, followed by a range of regulations and admonishments. A timetable of actions which caused changes to the agreed rules. He flipped through the pages annotated that he was nearing the end of the tome.

Toward the back was a laundry list of other titles which laid out details of incantations, magical actions which were considered either appropriate or unacceptable.

He slid his hand down the page, and squinted as he noted an indentation in the page. The shape of a nail.

Syphon Magicae. He tapped his foot on the floor. *Could it really be this simple?* Was it staring him in the face, and he'd not considered it? The description was clear; it was the magic of siphoning magic, for use by the person absorption. It also described the process of imbuing magic into a storage container for later access.

"Damn this," he muttered and rose, because now he'd need to find the *Tenebris Magicae Grimoire.* He remembered that book well, it was a deep red, the colour of blood, with dull copper clasps, and the title was kept in a secured storage zone.

Stalking the length of the room, he slid his hands down to his waist where he wore a belt with a long, black key. The lock screeched as the key turned, but it finally gave, and the door swung open.

Berith frowned seeing that the book layout was jumbled. He searched the appropriate row first, then high before crouching low. On the floor, slid beneath three other books, lay the *Tenebris Magicae Grimoire*, but the copper latches were broken.

"Damn you, Marrer," he muttered, snatching up the book. Practice had him relocking the secured storage before returning to the table and laying the book down.

It was instantly visible that the book had been desecrated, and he flipped through it, finding the torn section of book. Either side were descriptions of various incantations, which were the norm of grimoires.

He reopened the front of the book, checking to see if there was some kind of index, but none existed. "Not that I expected to find any," he growled.

Vinta came bounding down the centre of the room, having come from one of the smaller reading rooms. "Master, summoned Marrer," he uttered in a breathless manner. "Come now."

Berith frowned. "Why?"

Vinta stopped, cocked his head to the side. "No come?"

"What is she after?" A rhetorical question, of course. He shook his head. "No. I have an idea what it is she wants, and I'm not prepared to take a chance. Tell her that."

Vinta mewled. "She hurt me?"

Berith growled and reached into his pocket. "Take this." It was an amulet, one he'd been given after Fenella's abduction, though he had others. "Keep yourself safe, Vinta."

The smaller demon shook his head. "You need. Vinta go."

He reached out to grab his servant. "Take it. Use it. I have others."

Vinta blinked.

Rolling his eyes, Berith growled. "You know I trust you. I have no intention of leaving you in a position where you could be hurt or abducted. So, use it, for my peace of mind if for nothing else."

Reaching for the amulet, Vinta bobbed his head. "I take. I use."

"Good. By the way, who has access to the restricted books?" he queried.

"I not know. Vermeer know. I ask. Tell you."

It wasn't quite the answer Berith wanted, but he did trust Vinta to find out for him. For now, that would be enough.

Danu shook her head, finishing up with her daily work. It was hot, and she was sweating over the cauldron where she was disposing of the placenta of the woman she'd delivered.

It was one of the better tasks she'd undertake daily. Those who still believed in her were her priority, but it also wasn't unusual for her to be called to a case that was considered a very high risk.

"Lady, do you need anything?" Naamah hovered, a drink in her hand.

"Soon," she soothed, checking to confirm that every part was burned. She whispered as the smoke trailed into the air, ensuring mother and child recovered from the ordeal quickly. There were several important goddesses who'd assist at this time, but sacrifices were necessary to assure their help.

Satisfied, she rose and accepted the drink.

"Why do you not let others do this work?" queried Naamah.

"Because it is my task, and this final act of childbirth is important. Something that should be handled with care and love. It is my task and feeds my soul, Naamah."

"Do you not find it difficult? You are alone, and it's always been like that. Why do you not let others take this responsibility on? There are others who would attend this aspect and save your finer feelings."

Danu laughed, but the spoken arrow pierced her heart.

"But you have one you love, don't you?" Naamah frowned.

Danu was sure the oxygen was sucked out of her lungs. "I... I don't know what you're talking about." She headed toward the field, leaving her small chapel behind.

"Danu!" a voice boomed, and she looked up, gasping to see Berith striding toward her. He'd appeared in his full demon mode. His skin like ebony, eyes shining like miniature fires. The sight was breathtaking as much as heartbreaking.

She glanced down at herself, wishing she had time to change her appearance, but he'd already seen her. To change now… *Don't be stupid, it will look like you're concerned or embarrassed.* But that didn't mean she couldn't still wish.

"Berith, what brings you here?"

"I found the book, the one missing the page." He stared at her. "Am I interrupting your work?"

"Uh, no. I've just finished. One moment." She turned and saw Naamah skulking by the door. "Naamah, if you'd prepare our dinner. I won't be long."

She felt the heat of Berith's stare and turned slowly toward him. He was glowering at the demon. "What's she doing here? She's a minion of Marrer."

"Her sibling was. She never took an oath to your… mate." The word was distasteful to utter, but also true.

"She is no mate of mine," he growled, and for a moment, her heart stopped.

"Pardon?" She blinked.

"It was a mistake on my part, and one I hope to undo someday soon."

"Oh," she murmured. "Yes, I can see your problem. Go, Naamah," she said and shooed the demon to her home, waiting until the ripple of power told her that the demon had left them.

"You shouldn't trust her," Berith growled. "What if she attacks you in the night?"

Sighing, Danu shook her head. "She made her oath to me, Berith. You and I both know she can't do that if she'd bound to another. She stayed with Marrer until her sister died."

"Naheema?"

"Marrer killed her, then absorbed her power. That's what released Naamah, and she came to find me."

Berith grimaced. "You still shouldn't trust her."

"You never used to be so obstinate, Berith. Once she's given her fealty—and yes, I felt the power—she can't hurt me. I know that. You know that too. Now, tell me about the book."

He grunted. "Is my log still here?"

Danu stared at him. "Your log?"

"We're in the magic fields of *Hy-Brasail,* aren't we?"

She licked her lips. "Uh, yes." It was a good thing she'd not told Naamah to walk. That would make things a whole lot more difficult. After all, she'd never actually told Berith where she'd made her home. When they'd been…

"Danu?"

"Oh, uh log. Yes, it's still there. This island exists out of time, so it doesn't age."

He stared at her. "I know that. Now come. Let's go to the log and sit. I've missed this."

She shook her head, but stepped ahead of him, heading for the log at the very far edge of the field, shaded by a large oak tree, aware that he followed her. She was thankful he didn't speak, because her nerves quivered beneath the surface of her skin.

Once they'd made it to the log, she sat down, sighing as he took the spot beside her.

"I feel like it's been forever since we sat like this, Danu." His voice was soft, velvety. "Why did we stop?"

She opened her mouth then shut it again. She couldn't tell him, because that knowledge was bound by magic. She felt it swirling around him. For the first time she cursed the magic, because it dominated their lives, every aspect.

"Danu?" He turned to her, his hand reaching out in supplication. "What is it? Why are you so uncomfortable?"

If only she could tell him. She opened her hands wide. "Some things I do know and can't tell, and others I don't."

He frowned. "I don't remember you ever being so shy about telling me the truth. Did I do something so heinous that you hate me for it?" He raised a brow, and his red eyes glowed.

Berith stared at Danu and wondered where it had all gone wrong. His hand ached to take hers, the way they used to. His hand clutched hers.

"I've missed this," he muttered. He felt her tense. "I… You're restful," he murmured.

"That's not been my experience in the last century or two," she whispered. He wondered if she realised she'd spoken aloud but kept his counsel.

His fingers twined around hers, and he welcomed the warmth of her skin as the sun caressed them, and listened to the sound of birds singing in the trees. "I missed you, Danu."

"I hardly think so, Berith. You've continued to live your life."

"No, I truly have. My life has been tumultuous. Marrer…" How did he even begin to explain the confusion that engulfed him, thinking about the last period of time? It was as if something obstructed his memories, veiling them so he couldn't bring them forward.

"You shouldn't talk to me about your mate. It's not really the right thing to do."

Her words pulled him up, because, although she was right on one level, he valued her advice. He didn't understand why Marrer had changed so much since their mating. And of course, he certainly wasn't sure how it had come about when he considered the question. Even thinking about the situation made his head ache terribly.

"Thinking about it pains you," she said, squeezing his hands, and he glanced at her.

"You always knew," he said.

She shrugged.

"Balala…"

"Please, not today," she whispered, and her shoulders slumped.

He felt foolish as a wave of guilt crashed over him.

"Let's just enjoy the sun for a little longer," she said.

He hated that she seemed so lost, and he tugged her close, intending to hug her. But their gazes met. Hers was sad, and he moved, planning only to give her succour, to rest his forehead against hers, but they moved. He couldn't say how or why, just that suddenly his lips were on hers.

They were soft, plump.

She inhaled.

His lips parted.

The kiss was a gift, so delicate and yet full of meaning. She was still, not quite participating, but neither did she pull away. Thankful for the small mercy, he tugged back just enough to look into her eyes.

"Danu?"

She didn't speak or move. *What is she waiting for?*

"Please?"

She glanced down. "You have a mate, Berith. This cannot happen again." She whispered the words, eyes averted from him.

His guts twisted. "Is she? I don't know how it happened. I can't remember how it came to be. Why is that?"

When she closed her eyes, he ached. Her hand rose, cupping his cheek, and a tear trailed down her face before dropping from her chin. "There is no way I can help you. You took her to mate."

"But I don't remember, Danu." There was not just frustration but also confusion in his words. "I don't know how to fix this."

She opened her eyes and looked up, and there was misery in her gaze. "I don't... I can't help you. I..." She closed her mouth, but the trembling of her lips almost undid him. She shifted. "I have to go." And with a shake of her head, she was gone.

He sat for a moment, looking at the spot where she'd been. Sorrow poured into him, and he stood with a sigh. "I don't know what to do," he whispered to the air.

He returned to his home, but it was empty, bereft of any life.

6

Marrer stomped from one end of the room to the other. "Where has Naamah gone?"

The black-winged underling shook its head. "I don't know, mistress. Only that she left after Naheema... was consumed."

"She knows my secrets."

"Not all of them, Lady Marrer."

"Enough that she's a danger to me. Send someone to find her. And Vermuna? Make sure she is aware that crossing me is never tolerated." Marrer reclined on her throne, assured that Vermuna would find Naamah and ensure she died. Slowly. "I should have drained her when I consumed Naheema." It would have made life easier.

Now, if only she had access to the page. The whispers she'd heard had been enough to ensure her that it was a necessary aspect of her arsenal.

Even as she allowed her eyes to drift closed, a sound came from the doorway.

"Lady Marrer, I come with news." One of her generals, Orias, entered the room. His body was a bulk of muscles while the claws of his feet scraped on the floor.

"Orias, what do you have then to explain this intrusion?"

"News, Marrer. There is movement topside. A massing, if you will, by the sacred well."

The well was near the veil entry. An area she was barred from. An area she needed to control to complete her task. The subjugate all of humanity and wrest control from Berith as the effective second of Lucifer. Once she'd removed the stumbling block, then she could overthrow the fallen one and become the most powerful entity.

"When did this start?" she demanded, then stood and advanced on Orias, who quaked before her. She reached out and slid her hand down the face of the demon, her long, blood-red nail leaving a trail on his dark, leathery hide.

"My minions have indicated in the last week or so. I came as soon as they alerted me."

Her claws spread wide over his jugular, and he gulped, eyes wheeling in obvious fright, and the stink of terror was one she welcomed, would have bathed in, but she needed him and his troops. Only fear held his loyalty. "Indeed, and your minions… They are still watching?"

"Yes, Lady Marrer."

She pulled her hand away, noting the coating of sweat, licked it and found it was salty and pungent. It made her smile, and the warmth in her gut spread. "And you will continue to report any further activity?" she asked.

She glanced over her shoulder and noted with satisfaction that the demon nodded, the move convulsive and jerky.

"Good," she said. "Then, in appreciation of your actions, I will grant you a boon. Of my choosing, of course. Come, settle beside me." She patted the hard, stone seat next to her throne. "I find myself needing company. Companionship for the next short while."

She retreated to her chair, her body already sizing up how he might best service her needs. It had been far too long, and she positively ached for carnal satisfaction.

The demon moved slowly, as if sensing a trap. She didn't bother to contain the grin spreading across her face. After all, why should she? He was nothing more than a servant of her desires.

What was one other way to serve?

Now settled in her chair, she sighed. "I require stimulation, Orias. One only you can fulfill. For now, at least."

His eyes widened. "Lady Marrer?"

"Come, now. You have no mate, and mine…" She was careful not to utter any words that might bind her in any way to either Berith or Orias. The magic she'd used to hold Berith, to make him think he had taken a partners ritual, required that she must always be mindful and careful of the words she said aloud. "I have a need, as no doubt, so do you."

"But Berith," moaned Orias, and it was obvious the knowledge that she was being unfaithful to the one who believed himself to be her mate left him fearful.

"Have no concerns there, Orias. I will deal with him, when the time is ripe." And she would, in the fullness of time. But today and here was not the time or the place. And her body was clamouring for release. "But for now, come."

He scuttled forward, and containing her grin was beyond her ability.

The dream was torture to Danu.

"Berith," she said as he perched beside her on the log. "I…"

"I want to bind myself, Danu. The emotions inside me, they overwhelm me. Fill me and keep me warm."

Her eyes burned. "I wish…"

"Balala, she…" He cleared his throat. "The child… I loved her, Danu. But my loss, it left me so empty. I never thought another chance would come. I never expected to feel these emotions again."

"It's not been long, Berith. You need to heal."

"Haven't I?" He turned and his red eyes gazed into hers.

"I don't know. Have you?" Pain was tearing through her. Every word he said, a nail in the coffin of her own dreams.

"I have to go," he said, rising.

Her hands curled, wishing she could take his hand, stay him. But she didn't. Wouldn't. He didn't understand, and she wouldn't push that knowledge of him now. That wasn't fair, immaterial of how much it killed her. She told herself that such an action would be unwise to Berith. Instead, she inhaled, pasted a smile on her face, even though the fakery of it scored her.

"I… Good luck, Berith. I hope it's all you want and need."

He turned, and for a split second, there was an awareness in his gaze, then it slid away, replaced by the shining veil she'd seen recently. "Thank you, Danu. I'm sure we can continue to be friends."

"Friends," she parroted. But his offering speared her. It was so much less than she wanted or needed. She sucked in an unsteady breath, while her hands were clenched, tense in her lap.

Then he was gone, and she waited, her body a mass of aches, but it was the pain in her chest which felt like it was splitting her in two that dominated her thoughts. "Goodbye," she muttered. No matter what she might have told him, from this point on, preserving herself and her emotions was uppermost in her mind.

Danu woke, feeling the moisture on her cheeks. "I will not let this sorrow define me. I will overcome this."

She would help Berith to protect the humans, then she would retreat to her home. The time had come to let go of the farce that she was able to continue in her role.

She would hand over her responsibilities to the other goddesses of the pantheon. They would gladly accept them; after all, they'd all complained for centuries that she had too much power. "And that's what I will do. I'll need to make plans for Naamah too. I won't allow her to fade with me."

She rose, scooping up the candle beside her bed, and entered the kitchen. First, she'd make a coffee, then she'd make a list, detailing what plans need to be put in place.

Moments later, she settled at the table and began to make a list of what she needed to do, who should accept her obligations and rights.

The page filled quickly. She'd ensure the Dagda would care for Naamah and keep her safe. Ensure she had all she desired. Perhaps if she trained Naamah, she might even enter another goddess's service?

To Brigid she'd offer the followers of fertility. She'd also be a good fit to take on Naamah, maybe better than the Dagda, though she relied on the male to keep the demon safe. To Nantosuelta she would give abundance and magic along with nature. To Rhiannon she'd offer wisdom and motherhood.

Danu's home would be the place of her ending, and she planned to ensure that once she'd faded, it would close and fold itself into the aether. It would take a great amount of power, but she was prepared to expend that, given that she would be at the end of her time.

Sunlight reached its finger through the glass, and she inhaled, glancing down at the sheet of paper. She'd need to discuss her plans with the Dagda, to gain his assistance in preparing. That would be a vital aspect of her planning. For now, though, she lifted the pad and moved it into her bedroom. She was now assured that it would be safe until she was ready to declare her intentions, and she readied herself for the day ahead.

By the time Naamah emerged, Danu had a breakfast ready—coffee, eggs, and bacon. Thick peasant bread was rising by the oven, below her symbol of the triple spiral, and she was settled at the table, hands folded in her lap.

"You have breakfast?" Naamah queried.

"Yes. Sit down, and I'll serve it up."

Berith arrived at Fenella and Padraic's farm early, waited for the guards to contact Padraic, and waited until he was invited in. Rather like vampires, he was unable to cross thresholds until invited, and the fact that he was requesting the contact meant he arrived without ringing. Not that he could, given he owned no mobile phone of his own.

"Well, you've arrived early. Fenella was up last night with the babe," Padraic said by way of greeting, opening the door wide so Berith could enter the house.

"You've been busy," commented Berith. He remembered the last time he'd been here; the house and lands had been in disarray. The structure ramshackle and the gardens overgrown.

"Aye, Fenella has been important in deciding how to recreate what was here before."

"As you remembered it?" Berith queried.

"Aye, but my visits here before had always been intermittent. And while the family itself who lived here previously weren't blood, Fenella takes the history of the property very seriously, given they were the family of her heart."

Fenella's mother had been compelled by a demon and had conceived Fenella from the dalliance, before returning to the man who truly loved her. He'd taken on the child, loved her, parented her, and raised her as if she were his own. It was a secret which both parents had kept even to the grave, and when Marrer had attempted to gain control of the property, that had been an aspect which had come to light.

"She's handling the knowledge well?"

"She's working with Vinta and others to learn about her powers, how to cope with them. The babe, though, was a trial. She wasn't sure what would happen, but all is well now."

"Then I'm pleased for you. And your daughter? Genevieve?"

Padraic smiled. "The wedding was lovely. It's a shame you were unable to attend. Genny did hope you may have been able to, but she understood. David's entire family was in attendance."

Genny had been conceived of a lycan and hidden for years. Padraic had only recently become aware of his police officer daughter's existence in New York. *The tentacles of magic have a long reach.* Of course, then there was also David's family and his connections to highly ranked vampires, as the women were consorts of heads of vampire houses.

"Good. Good," Berith said.

"Tea?" Padraic offered, and Berith nodded his acceptance, following the leprechaun through the house to the kitchen.

"Thank you." He settled into the chair Padraic indicated to. "I wanted to know how your planning was going. When are Luke and Grace due to arrive?"

Padraic filled the kettle from the sink, lit the burner on the stove, and set the kettle over the flame, then wandered over to the table. "We've been organising the teams to mass near the well. I got control of the property years ago, so that's not a problem. We have reports that Marrer's people are watching, so none of this is covert." Then he sat down.

"No, I didn't really expect it to be." Berith tapped his cheek. "I dare not head over there just yet, and I have other priorities for the moment, including trying to get Lucifer to agree to return to the underworld."

Padraic quirked a brow. "He's not there?"

Berith sighed. "No. He's been absent for a very long time, something I've been working to keep quiet, because…" He shrugged. "It doesn't do for news that the Lord of the Underworld is in seclusion and has been for centuries."

Padraic leaned forward, clasping his hands together. "So who's been in charge?"

Berith sighed. "That's the problem. No one really. That's what has allowed Marrer's influence to grow."

Padraic rose and went about pulling the kettle from the hob and pouring water into the pot. Then he carried it, returned to the side, and grabbed two mugs and teaspoons. "No sugar or milk, right?"

Berith shook his head. "Hot, black tea is soothing."

"What else is bothering you?" Padraic's question surprised Berith.

"What do you mean?"

Padraic sat back. "You forget, I've known you for centuries. Not well, until recently, but still…" He sipped his tea. "You talk about soothing, you're more unbent, and yet you also seem scattered. So I know something's on your mind."

Berith sighed. It wasn't like he had many to talk to. If Lucifer had been present… "I've a problem. Marrer—"

"Your mate?"

Berith nodded. "I can't remember the ritual of mating. I remember when Balala and I... but it's strange. It's like there's something I can see and that doesn't seem right."

Padraic placed his drink on the table. "Is there a chance you might not be mated?"

Berith's mouth opened. "I... I don't know. That would mean she was controlling me. Compelling me. That needs a deep and heavy magic."

"Aye, and one would need a well of magic to complete that."

A thought occurred to Berith, and it shook him. "I need to see Danu," he muttered.

Padraic nodded. "When you need me, I'll be here."

7

Danu felt the second Berith arrived. A tingle in the air, which was rapidly followed by, "I need your help," his voice thick and shaking.

"What's wrong?" She turned and stared at him. He'd taken on human form, and she couldn't miss the worry that wrinkled his brow.

"You know the gods and goddesses better than me." He ran a shaking hand through his hair, and she wanted to soothe him.

"I... Yes."

"Have any disappeared, or faded, in the last three or four centuries?"

She sighed heavily and laid down the cloths she'd been folding, preparing for another delivery of her own. "A few. Mostly lesser gods or goddesses, but I don't really associate all that much..." And she didn't. Too many remembered her as a far more happy individual and some still queried... She shook her head. "Ate is the one that comes to mind. She was fading because she'd lost many of her followers."

"Ate? She was the goddess of war?"

"No," Danu corrected. "Lies, delusions, and so on. A daughter of Zeus, but he spent little time with her, and regularly scolded her. She encourages recklessness and self-destruction."

His gut knotted. "Can you remember when?"

She did remember, clearly. It was before Marrer but after the loss of Balala. "Just before you mated with Marrer," she answered. She hated saying the words, but when his eyes closed, she leaned forward, touching his hand. "What's wrong?"

"Tell me what you know about the fading."

Her heart ceased beating for long seconds before she accepted he had no idea of her plans. "I... It's simple. We relinquish what power we still possess. It's accepted that we apportion our responsibilities to others, then we find our safe place to retreat, and we cease to be. Simply let time and magic drift away." She whispered the last words, because while she'd accepted her fate, hearing the steps was confronting.

"Could she be a prisoner?"

Danu blinked. "I guess. At that time, we're usually alone. Weak and vulnerable. Once we release our magic, we have no defences."

"And if you were Marrer?"

His query had her pausing. "You need to see Zeus if that's the case. She's his daughter, and it would be him that would need to release her. It would take something I don't have, or even our pantheon. A direct genetic link."

"I also need to get Zazrael. He's weak. Ineffectual. Oh, he may well be Marrer's second, but that's because she doesn't want anyone too strong near her. Someone who could overthrow her," he muttered.

"How do you plan to do that?" While Danu could see the benefit of what he said, the actual task would be harder. Wouldn't it? Unless... "Let me try."

He advanced. "No," he said, shaking his head, his face dark and tight.

"No, listen for a moment, Berith. He would be wary of you and cagey. But what would he expect from me? I'm not truly aligned to you." How saying those words hurt! "If he's not a planner, or even strong, he won't expect anything. I can lure him."

Berith's lips tightened, brackets of white appearing. "It's too dangerous."

She shook her head. "Not at all. There's a gathering tomorrow morning. The Festival of Light sees both sides gathering. There's no reason I can't do my thing…" She twirled a little and gave a grin.

He growled. "No, Danu. We'll find another way."

She sighed, because he'd be difficult now. The best option was to dive in quickly. Attend to the task while he wasn't watching. She'd just have to give Naamah a job, so she didn't appear at Danu's side. That would destroy the illusion that she was somehow unaligned. She was relying on Marrer's secretive nature, even from her brother.

"Look, let's leave the discussion for a day or two, right? I have tasks I need to complete and…" A chime, muted but insistent, echoed through the small chapel. "I must go. I'm being summoned to a difficult birth of one of my followers."

He frowned. "Will you promise…?"

She smiled, avoiding the question, then blinked away.

Berith hated when she did that but accepted her disappearance. Naamah wandered into view. "Naamah?"

"Yes, Lord Berith?"

"Stay with her. She's… I fear there's danger brewing, and I would hate for her to be caught in the middle." It was less than he wanted to say, but the binds of matehood still kept him from understanding why her safety was paramount to him.

Naamah searched his gaze. "You care for her?"

He started. "I… yes."

She gave a nod. "You need to keep her safe. Marrer is wicked. She has secrets. Many, many secrets. Hidden places. Some of them I've seen, and others… There are whispers in the underworld that she has a place so hidden that only she and Zazrael know. It is the source of her power over you."

"Where?" demanded Berith.

She shrugged. "That I don't know. But Zazrael would."

Berith grunted. "I need to find him."

"He likes the cemeteries, but Marrer only releases him now and again. I think she fears that time alone would endanger him, and by default, her standing in the underworld."

"Any in particular?" he queried.

"No. It makes him difficult to find. But he particularly likes moonless nights. Now, I must go. I must assist Danu, otherwise she overtaxes herself."

He frowned at that. "Overtaxes?"

Naamah sighed, shrugged. "She's weaker than she lets you know. She's at risk, my lord."

"Go," he growled, suddenly understanding the gravity of Danu's situation.

Danu walked across the grass; for all intents and purposes, the highly strung and nasty goddess she'd projected. Her hair was coiled in dark red ringlets, and her gown was a pure white, deceptively simple, which displayed her assets deliciously, with a slim belt around her slender waist.

She glanced carefully left and right, looking for Zazrael in the massed demonic ranks. He stood out at the edge of the crowd, swarthy and rough, his attire of black leather unadorned. She sighed, wondering how best to attract his interest.

The pantheon had formed their ranks, only missing her, and she moved slowly, picking her way over the damp grass. Every step carefully choreographed, and she felt the heat of his gaze. The interest. It made her skin crawl, but she'd set herself a task, and by heavens, she'd complete it.

She was the last of the light to join in, but she gave all she had, welcoming the warming sun. The solstice was an important date, and the Festival of Light was a pivotal annual event, welcoming the high summer before the slow and steady descent into winter. It was the point at which the underworld relinquished control of the lands until the next solstice. That of the darkness.

"I thought you'd never catch up," muttered Rhiannon on her left.

Danu smiled sweetly. "Oh, I like to take my time," she answered gaily, and the Dagda admonished her with a frown.

Rhiannon tittered behind her hand as she focussed on their obeisance to the orb of the sun.

"We welcome you, great light. We welcome these long days of growth and plenty," they called out in unison.

Sun warmed the earth, and finally they were done. Rhiannon tried to catch Danu's eye, but she floated away before any could invite her to join them. Escaping into the field, which appeared empty behind them, though she knew she was watched from the woods.

She took careful steps, trying to appear natural, while moving with slow grace, hoping she'd caught his eye. Then suddenly he was there. Zazrael made his way toward her smoothly, for all his bulk.

"You are alone, fair Danu," Zazrael growled.

"Indeed, demon. What do you want of me?" This was the most dangerous time for her, and she'd need to navigate with care. Hopefully, he'd come when she summoned him.

"Words for now, goddess," he muttered. "I have no mate and seek one."

She quirked her brow. "And you consider who?"

"You are weakened. You need power, and I… I desire more than I have."

"Yes," Danu answered. "And you think I would make a suitable mate?" She kept her voice low, though horror laced her gut.

"My sister, she demands I submit, but she has secrets. She has power, but only that which she steals. Not of her own, and she has inveigled Berith. He believes she mated him."

Danu's breath stilled. "He didn't? That would take a lot of power to make him think so." She laughed, hoping she sounded honest in her mirth. "I doubt Marrer could…"

Zazrael leaned toward her, and the scent of brimstone had nausea rising. She controlled it—barely. "She keeps a goddess in her grasp." He grinned, jagged teeth and fiery red eyes alerting her to the danger she now faced.

"Indeed," whispered Danu, sliding her hand down to her waist, fumbling for the sticky net she'd secreted there in the hopes that this would occur. "Tell me more," she whispered, leaning in, and with a deft manoeuvre, tossed the magical web at the demon. It stuck, and while he tried to claw it off, she inhaled before letting out a magical cry of "Berith! Come urgently."

He appeared, his face black with thunder. "What have you done?" he demanded, stalking toward her.

"I told you—"

"Stupid woman! I told you to wait!" Berith bellowed, his chest heaving as he raged. "Will you never learn?"

She shrank back, noting the fury, and scalded by it. "I was helping…"

"Have you no sense of self-preservation? It's no wonder you're fading!" His words pierced her chest. Cold barbs that sank deep. Tore at her psyche and sense of worth.

"I…" Her hands shook, and she clutched them tight to her breast. "I wanted to help."

She felt confused and lost and so hurt! Inside her ached, and it was like something deep within was splintering. Cracking open. Tears burned, but she blinked them away. Now was not the time, she told herself, because if she released her control on her emotions, they might well drown her.

"All you've done is endanger you and everyone around you," he snarled with brutal frigidity.

She opened her mouth and closed it again. What could she say? All she'd wanted to do was assist him. "He knows her secrets. About you," she muttered, drawing herself up, dragging the cloak of self-sufficiency around herself. "I will relieve you of my presence," she said with a cold formality she'd practiced over centuries, then closed her eyes and willed herself away.

"Ah, so now I understand!" Zazrael laughed.

Berith turned toward Zazrael and noted the web which Zazrael was plucking at. Berith fashioned magical manacles from the air and slid them onto the demon before Zazrael could disappear. Danu had expended a large amount of energy on fashioning the web, and he refused to allow her actions to be for nothing. He already regretted his harsh outburst. He'd just…

"Like that too?" Zazrael laughed. "Poor Berith and Danu. Star and love crossed," snorted the demon.

Grabbing the other by the arm, Berith punched at the air, and they were in a small cavern. Protected from time and prying eyes. A place Marrer could not find, and laid out perfectly for his needs, Berith thought. He pushed Zazrael against the wall and coils of magically infused cord held the demon close.

"So now it's time to answer my questions," Berith snarled.

"Uh, are you sure?" Zazrael grinned. "You might have me in a dungeon and all, but… I can still run." He tried lifting one leg, then the other, the movements of his hips betraying him. "What have you…" snarled the demon before him.

Berith chuckled. "Serpentine?" A hissing filled the air, and from the wall emerged a long snake. "So glad you were able to join me, and so quickly." He'd warned her he may need her assistance sometime soon, though not quite yet.

His mind flashed to an image of Danu's shocked features, but he banished the memory. He'd deal with her later.

Behind Zazrael, the snake hissed in a menacing fashion. "Let me introduce you to my little friend—Serpentine. She's not very well-known, but you've heard of her, haven't you? She's neither goddess nor demon and answers only to herself. A magical kind of being, if you will." Berith snapped his fingers, and a chair appeared before the wall, where Zazrael was now held. "She's very special, but you know that too. Don't you?"

Zazrael's eyes rolled. He quivered, and Berith wished he could take joy in the sight, but there was no pleasure to be found. Serpentine owed him a favour, and he was calling in many right now, to get to the bottom of Marrer's dangerous plot and ultimately to destroy her and the army she'd built.

"So, tell me, does Marrer truly have control over me?" Berith said.

Zazrael opened then closed his mouth, face reddening. "I'm bound," he sputtered.

Berith cocked his head. "Bound? Hmm, let's try again then. Verbal only?"

Zazrael squirmed, clearly attempting to free himself from the situation, but Berith had prepared this cavern long ago with Lucifer. He knew the depths of the magic and knew that only Lucifer could undo the multitude of incantations which imbued this room.

"I… I won't answer," he snarled.

Serpentine twined around him, hissing her displeasure and moving herself so she could stare into the demon's eyes. "Answer him, or I bite," she demanded. "My venom will compel you, but if I use it, it will burn for a thousand years. Like you are cooking from the inside out."

Zazrael's eyes moved in his direction and Berith nodded. "I hear it's a most unpleasant experience."

The demon closed his eyes. Fury and terror were present, the ripe scent filling Berith's nostrils, while he detected the rhythmic clenching of fists.

"Come, Zazrael, save yourself the pain and anguish," Berith said. "A thousand years, and during that time, you'll remain hidden in here, while you pay the price of your intransigence. Dear me," he muttered.

Serpentine moved forward, her tongue licking the air. "Maybe a small demonstration," she offered, and the flesh swiped over Zazrael's. He howled in pain, and Serpentine drew back. "Urgh, revolting creature," she mumbled.

Moments passed as Zazrael shook and cried out, but, as serpentine had merely tasted and left saliva on the demon's skin, the pain appeared to pass quite quickly. He and Serpentine gave Zazrael time to recover. Berith lounged on the chair, tapping his long, black fingers against the wood of the arms, waiting for the chance to ask the question again.

Zazrael inhaled, the sound unsteady, but it was enough to make Berith smile. He was ready to try again. "Well, Serpentine, I think it's time to ask again," murmured Berith. The hiss that emerged from Zazrael told him that the demon was aware he was in total control of the situation. "So, I take it the compulsion your sister set on you is verbal only?"

The demon writhed, and it was clear the compulsion was painful, but when he screamed, "stop!" while nodding in agreement, it also told Berith that Serpentine's venom was far more powerful.

"Good. Does she have Ate?"

Zazrael's nod was slow, laboured. But it told Berith what he needed to know.

"Can you show me the way to where Marrer is holding her?"

This time Zazrael shook his head, while sobbing, piteously arching against the pain which Berith assumed lashed him.

"Well, Zazrael. I'm not letting you go yet. After all, Marrer will want to make you pay, and I don't think I have all the answers I deserve just yet. So, Serpentine, I thank you for your assistance, but hope you will return when I'm ready to begin again?"

Serpentine uncoiled herself and slithered to the floor before assuming human form. Her hair was jet-black, and she was of short stature with almond-shaped eyes. Her clothing of tight, black pants and a peasant-style shirt was completed with black, ankle-length boots. "I wouldn't miss it for all the world," she answered, her voice plummy English, then she disappeared from view.

Berith stalked toward the demon, noting the pallor and streaks on his cheeks. "I'll be back soon, Zaz. But for now, think on my questions. Oh, and you can call for your sister, but the cavern is protected by Lucifer himself. She will not gain entry, nor will you escape."

The bound demon quaked. "Don't... Don't leave me here," cried Zazrael, but Berith only grunted before he returned to his home.

8

anu's trepidation rose. After Berith's brutal swipe, she was done. It was time to meet with the Dagda and plan her fading.

"Naamah? I've got tasks to undertake today that you cannot join me on. Enjoy the day."

Naamah's gaze followed her. "Why not?"

"It's Tuatha business, which means you can't attend. You can stay here and do whatever. Cook or sew or read… Anything you like," she answered, pasting on what she hoped was an easy smile.

She couldn't tell if Naamah accepted it at face value, but right now, she was aching. Soul weary, and just needed to end it all.

"I'll be here when you return then," the demon answered.

"Fine. Yes, and when I return, we can discuss the evening meal. But for now…" Danu smiled and nodded before time and place wrapped around her.

Stepping into the Dagda's meeting room was a shock. She'd not been here in many years, and to see the changes — including a wall of computers and the room lit by sunlight filtered through long panes of glass framed by heavy block-out curtains — surprised her. The long table of oak and the chairs around the table brought back memories of them meeting to plan their efforts.

Today she felt a pang of sadness, looking to the four empty seats, others who'd faded to become one with the universe. She ran her fingers along the backs of the chairs. Soon, her chair would be vacant. She bit her lip.

"Why did you call this meeting, *a chara*?" Rhiannon asked, stepping up to her.

"It's time," she simply said.

Morrigan took her spot at one end of the table, the Dagda took the other, and the seats were filled.

Dagda frowned at Danu. "This isn't an easy option, child."

She nodded. "I know. But I've considered the reality. I'm weak now. My magic has waned, and I'm fading. So I need to—"

"Have you considered taking a mate?" Morrigan queried.

Glancing down the length of the table, Danu nodded. "I have. But since…" She shrugged.

"Berith never understood what you gave up for him," Macha growled. "I should have run—"

"Enough!" Cailleach muttered. "He was ever Danu's choice."

Danu's hands were clasped together. "I've thought long and hard, my friends. When we were cast out of Nemed, we promised, all of us, never to drain our resources. But of all, I'm the one who's never found a mate. And we know that is imperative to stabilising the power drain."

Aengus Og smiled. "Love is everywhere. Why, I could find you—"

"No," Danu said with a shake of her head. "I have loved. I lost it, and it's right I pay the price for my pride."

"You've considered the fate of your followers?" Morrigan queried.

"I have," Danu answered. "There are many who are compatible, so I've created a plan to assist my followers to find and follow another."

Lugh cleared his throat. "I am certain you have made all the necessary plans, but I would ask you wait. Until after this looming battle we need to table this discussion. However, there is other news, and things that must be discussed today."

She bit her lip, understanding Lugh's concerns. "I will, but when it's done, I would ask that you all assist. I need to make sure Naamah is settled and cared for. Safe. I need to be sure that there are those who would watch over my priests. Care for them and theirs, as I've done for centuries."

Murmurs ran the length of the table, but it was Aine who raised a hand to gain control of the discussion. "I would ask that you feel at ease in changing your mind, should the opportunity rise."

Danu sighed and nodded. "Indeed, I shall remember that, but I fear the time has come to be honest with myself and you all."

The Dagda cleared his throat. "So, once the battle is completed, we shall reconvene. For now, though, I have news. From the otherworld."

All turned toward him, and Danu was pleased she was no longer the topic of conversation.

"Indeed," said Lugh.

"It appears that the demon Marrer had tried to open a portal to the world. It may be necessary for us to send an envoy back to the other-world to—"

"They have asked for that?" Morrigan queried, brow wrinkled.

Dagda laughed, the sound harsh. "Not exactly. Not yet, but my communications have certainly raised concerns that if she can travel there, or send demons through…"

"It would be a bloodbath," Cailleach said.

Danu wanted to say it couldn't happen, but all gathered around the table knew the truth. The otherworld was incapable of protecting itself, as their strongest, brightest, and those who understood, had all been sent away.

"How will you communicate the danger?" she asked, then tried to scrunch down in her seat because she hadn't wanted to claim any further attention.

"We can't," Morrigan answered. "The powers that be, they never trusted us, and they would hardly do so now. They knew we were aware of the many weaknesses of the otherworld's defences. Their lack of understanding of their magics, and of course, the weaknesses of their leadership, were of concern to them. They were only some of the reasons we were expelled. We knew all too well how to harness and use our magic, and that made us a threat. The young who learned from us, as you did, Danu, was a threat to their echelons of power. They think that they've been successful because they don't want to know the truth."

Naamah smiled with pleasure as she stripped the bed and remade it with fresh sheets. That Danu had taken her into her service was a pleasure that she had every intention of repaying. For a demon, and a minion of Marrer—even if she hadn't given her oath—it was something she could only have dreamed of. She was now sure that Danu was indeed the kindest of goddesses. Others saw the façade she presented to the world, but for Naamah, it was like being allowed into an inner sanctum.

So, since Danu was attending a meeting of the Tuatha, it occurred to Naamah that cleaning the house was a simple way to thank the goddess. She gathered the items that had been placed into a hamper of dirty clothes, and looked around for anything else before heading for the old-fashioned laundry. After placing the clothes into the washing machine, Naamah returned to the bedroom, planning to dust the small dressing table in the corner.

She lifted each item, swiping away any motes before replacing the item where it had been found. Behind a small candlestick, Naamah found a folded piece of paper. She slid it to the side of the dressing table as she cleaned the holder, and it fluttered to the floor.

She reached down for the paper, noting that the page had unfurled. Her eyes caught the words, '*fading.*' Naamah frowned. "What's this?"

It took a moment for the meaning of the sheet to take hold, and she gasped.

"She's planning her fade." It had her guts seizing. "How can she do this?"

She dropped to sit on the floor, cradling the sheet.

"What do I do?"

A sound echoed from the room beyond. She swiped at her eyes and lumbered to her feet. "Danu?" a voice called, and with shock, she realised it was male...

She knew the voice. It was Berith. She hurried from the room, not realising she still held the sheet of paper in her hand.

"Berith!" Naamah called.

He turned and looked at her.

It worked, Berith thought, pleased that his theory worked. He planned to talk with Danu, explain his fury...

He came face-to-face with Naamah, who was white-faced and teary. "What's wrong? Where's Danu?" His heart thudded fast. Was it possible she could be hurt?

"I... How did you get here?" she stuttered.

"I followed the energy from the last time she summoned me," he answered, glancing around. *Where is Danu?*

"Oh," Naamah muttered. "Danu... She's..." He noted the fear in her eyes, and dread chilled him to the core.

"Is she hurt?" His fingers clenched into tight fists.

"No," Naamah whispered, voice shaking as much as her head. "She..." Naamah shoved a piece of paper at him. "She's planning her fading," she breathed.

Naamah's words were a punch to the gut. He blinked, knowing he'd hurt her with his intemperate words. He'd been harsh and reactive. He couldn't banish the shock that ricocheted through him, nor forget the look on her face. He felt as if he'd somehow betrayed her.

He glanced at the paper and reeled physically. Reached out to find a support, because what he saw written down terrified him. Her plans were clear, her delegation of responsibilities apparent. Her hurt had been deeper than he realised.

She was preparing to cease to be.

Gone from this world and every other one.

"I will not allow this," he growled.

Naamah's eyes widened. "You have no hold on her, my lord. Your mate…"

He shook his head, cutting off any words Naamah might utter. "This will not come to be, but for now, put it back where you found it, then we must plan."

Waiting while Naamah disappeared, Berith considered the situation. Things were fraught, they needed to defeat Marrer, and he'd messed everything up with Danu.

Naamah returned. "What do we do?"

"Act like normal. I'll talk to her." *If she'll listen to me, that is.* Perhaps he needed to ask… He shook his head. Danu was insular, uncomfortable talking about her personal issues with others, so if he brought others into the discussion, she'd be harder to help.

A sudden ripple filled the air.

"She's here," breathed Naamah.

He nodded. "Act natural," he reminded the demon and waited for Danu to appear.

Danu's eyes widened on him as she realised his presence. "You. What are you doing in my home, Berith? I didn't invite you, nor summon you. So how…?"

He shook his head, trying to consider why he was here. "Zazrael admitted Marrer has Ate. I haven't yet found where she's being held."

"I see. I should inform the Dagda." Danu nodded as if she'd made some great discovery, but remained remote in her manner, keeping herself aloof. "You should go now." She started to raise her hand, her symbol that she was ready to leave.

Before she could disappear, Berith snatched her hand. "Wait," he muttered.

She cocked her head to the side. "You're holding onto me." The words were carefully enunciated.

"Yes."

"Why?"

"I need to talk to you, Danu."

"Me? I don't think so, Berith. Now, if you'll excuse me?" She stared at his hand holding onto her, but he didn't release her. "Berith?"

"I was wrong," he muttered.

She quaked, but her head snapped up. "Whatever. Let me go."

He shook his head. "We need to talk."

Her mouth tightened. "Later. Let me go so I can let the Dagda know."

Berith realised he wasn't going to get any further right now. But before he released her, he leaned in. "We will talk, Danu."

She sneered, then thrusting her hand upright, she was gone.

Naamah peeked around the corner. "What are you going to do? She sounded really pissed with you."

He hadn't missed that either. He sighed. "I don't know just yet. But I will sort this out." But in his gut, he wasn't so sure.

9

Berith marched into the cave and noted that Zazrael was hanging limply. Blood streaking down his flanks.

"Serpentine?" Berith called.

She appeared, eyes dark, though her lips were ruby red, and the colour of her skin was flushed. "I have news, Berith. Come."

They stepped up to Zazrael, who roused slightly, eyes only a little open. "You came back," he whispered.

"Serpentine called me. You know something I need to know?"

Zazrael coughed, the sound weak and damp. "Yeah, Ate... Marrer has mostly absorbed her essence. She's..." He coughed again, and a bright dribble of scarlet flowed from his mouth.

Berith listened, and in his gut, a heavy boulder of fear rose.

Danu strode into the house, shaking her head. The meeting with Dagda had been fraught, because he'd demanded information. Things she didn't know. Now, thoroughly out of sorts, all she wanted to do was bathe, eat, then go to bed.

Naamah hovered. "I've cooked dinner for you, Danu."

Indeed, she had. The scent filled the air, and Danu's stomach gurgled. "Let me bathe first, then I'll join you." She needed the privacy and sanctity of her room right now. Somewhere to lick her wounds.

Berith's presence earlier had scoured her, because he didn't understand the depths of her despair, so she sailed past the demon, though taking care to glance at her and smile.

She used just enough energy to magic a bath, deep and filled with steamy, floral-scented water, and closed the door behind her. Shrugging off her clothes, she advanced then slid into the water. Taking a moment to breathe, she let the echoes of roses and lavender fill her senses. He'd brought her roses, all those years ago, when they'd met in the meadow. "I'm getting lost in my past," she muttered.

So many times, she'd hoped for more, but nothing had come to pass. She'd follow through on what she'd agreed to, then she'd let the aether decide. Danu sighed and rose, reaching for the towel, and set about dressing quickly.

Trailing to the kitchen, she sat down and Naamah set the meal before her. Corned meat with vegetables. A good hearty, though basic, meal. "Thank you for this, Naamah."

The demon settled opposite her, steepling her fingers as Danu watched. "It's the least I could do, given you've taken me under your wing."

Danu bit her lip. She'd accepted the demon's fealty, and yet she was planning to pass her along, like a chattel. The demon deserved better, only, how did she give her freedom without condemning her to a life of fearing Marrer, Zazrael, and their followers?

"If you were not here, what would you rather do with yourself?" Danu asked. "I mean, demons have long lives, and by my reckoning, you're still young."

The demon blushed heavily. "Do you not want me here?"

Danu sighed, wishing she could be honest with the woman. She was coming to consider Naamah a friend, and it wasn't like she had lots of them. Or even a confidante. "It's not that I don't want you here, but you deserve better than this." She bit her lip. "But I do want to know more about you. About your dreams and desires. I want to help you achieve them."

"I was born a demon, but that has implications, Lady Danu. Ones I can't escape." Naamah dropped her head and shook it before glancing back up. "Demons are bad, wicked and ugly." Naamah looked at her. "That's what most people think of us, but we aren't. Not really. Well, not all of us anyway. We are manacled by our natures, and avoiding it, is fraught. But me? I want a chance to be more. I'd like to find a lover. Maybe a husband and children, if I'm lucky. I want to have a family and a future." Her lips trembled and that moved Danu.

Naamah's words reminded her that loss of hope was crushing. "No, not all demons are bad. Some can and do rise above the role that is predetermined for them. I can see that in you."

Berith too, whispered her brain.

She took a bite as her mind whirred.

"Danu!" The frisson of magic washed over her, and she rose, turned as Berith stumbled into the kitchen. "Come quick!"

"What?" Her hand clutched to her breast as she stared at the demon, his skin gleaming in the candlelight she preferred at night.

"Zazrael has confessed where Ate is being held. But time is limited. He said Marrer is planning to finish draining her. We need to mass forces. The Dagda…"

"Naamah, you should stay here," Danu said. "I don't want you caught in the crossfire."

She was already preparing herself mentally, and with a wave of her hand, dressed in a full black combat suit, hair ruthlessly contained in a braid. At her waist was a sword, a vicious Hallstatt she'd owned for centuries. The sword had an intricate hilt, inlaid with garnet, and the scabbard continued the theme and a triple spiral symbol etched into it.

"I'll be back," she bit out and moved through space so she arrived at the Dagda's home.

He was sitting in his chair, in pyjama bottoms, a tray on his lap, with a meal and a glass of wine. "Danu?" He straightened up.

"Berith is in my home. He knows where Ate is, and she's in Marrer's clutches. She's dying, Dagda. Needs us and our help."

The tray was gone in an instant, and Dagda pulled himself up to stand, now clothed like her, for war.

"We need the others," he muttered.

"Aye. But we need to go now." She rubbed her brow. "Meet in the meadow?"

Dagda nodded and she exhaled.

"I'll be quick as I can," he answered.

Satisfied she'd done all she could, she spirited herself back to her home, where Berith waited, pacing back and forth until he turned and saw her.

"We're to meet in the meadow," she told him. "Come, I'll take you."

His gaze quirked. "I can take both of us."

She sighed, frustrated and irritated by equal measure. "No. I... There's a shortcut. But one only I know."

His lips thinned, and she took his hand.

They stepped together as one, then another step and they were in the field.

"Impressive," he said. "But I could have..."

She rolled her eyes as quickly as she dropped his hand and stepped away. "No. Now I need time to prepare," she muttered and dragged the sword from its scabbard and started to move through a series of action. Each move warming her muscles and testing to ensure she was ready for the battle ahead.

The stretches gave her a chance to quiet the sudden noise in her mind, as she pushed back the awareness of him, the way her entire body tingled.

She knew he watched, felt the heat of his gaze, but with each action, she breathed easier, and her limbs reacted a little more smoothly.

One by one, the others joined them, as did a contingent of Berith's demons.

Dagda pushed to the front, and Danu let him, not wishing to be a leader in what was to come. When Berith snapped his fingers, Zazrael appeared, leashed by a woman of Asian appearance. She had long, black hair and almond-shaped eyes, but it was the claws holding the metal chain connected to Zazrael's hands that caught Danu's attention. The silver ring in the shape of a snake, with matching emerald eyes which gleamed in the sunlight.

"Serpentine," she muttered, remembering the creature from times past. When Balala had been alive.

Berith waited for silence, then raised his hands. He'd assumed his human persona and clothed himself in heavy leather pants and a jacket, the sword at his side one he'd been given by Lucifer himself. The burn at the core, banked until they were in battle, then the length would flame and score its marks.

He shook Dagda's hand when it was extended. "Ye know where Ate is being held?" the god demanded.

"I do indeed," he answered. "But Zazrael is our passage there." Berith cleared his throat. "We must all form a chain, hold onto one another to make the transition." It appeared that only when in direct contact with either of the two 'makers of the cavern' could they enter.

Danu had shifted to the back of the pack, so he stalked toward her and took her hand. "My partner," he muttered.

She blinked. "Take Dagda's hand instead," she hissed, but he shook his head.

"No. You, come."

She acquiesced soundlessly, and he wished there was time to grip onto the pleasure, but time was waning for Ate, so instead he dragged her forward, forcing the others to form a chain of beings. Serpentine hissed and released Zazrael as Berith took one hand while still gripping Danu with the other.

"Take us," Berith ordered, and Zazrael whimpered.

The magic was cloying and sickly; the pungent aroma of musk and scorched flesh battered him for long seconds before they were in the cavern. Serpentine, her grip on his shoulder, regained control of the chains keeping Zazrael their prisoner.

"Show us," Berith demanded, and Zazrael lurched forward, past the remains of others who'd been sucked dry of their magic, bodies littering the ground and still held in their bonds.

No one spoke, the unsaid agreement of silence eery in the flickering light of the torches. Feet moved carefully, but there was still the crunch as they moved toward the end of the tunnel.

A room came into view, and within the lit room was a suspended woman, her red hair lank, the robes limp and loose.

"Ate," whispered Danu.

The room didn't appear to hold anyone else, but before the Dagda could take a step, Danu held out a hand. "There's a ward," she muttered.

Her hands extended, and he wondered what she could feel. "Danu?"

"Zazrael knows how to clear it," she said, her voice low. "If we attempt to cross it, it will call forth minions. Let him go first."

Serpentine laughed softly. "I'll take him," she offered.

Danu shook her head. "No. Berith, Serpentine's magic is incompatible. Marrer has used some kind of familial magic here."

Berith frowned. "Familial?"

"It's what allows him to come and go. Isn't that right, Zazrael? The link is an emotional bond, so he must be the one to open the way. But I can control him through the chain. Let me take him through."

"Not without me," Berith growled. Fury that she'd take a risk like that singed his mind. "I'll come with you."

"I don't know if that's safe," she muttered, but let him grab her arm as she took control of Zazrael.

They stepped through in sequence, Zazrael, then Danu gripping the chains in sweaty hands, while Berith gripped her shoulder.

The wash of cold as they passed the wards was unnerving, but once within, she passed the chains holding Zazrael and hurried toward Ate, sure that at any second a horde of Marrer's minions would descend.

"Ate, I'm here to release you," she whispered to the clearly depleted goddess. From her left boot, Danu drew a small knife and sliced at the leather bonds, then Ate sagged at her.

Berith was there, taking her from Danu and rising up. "We should get out of here," he muttered, and she wanted to say 'no, really?' but she knew time was now of the essence.

"Well, Zaz, I guess you did the job after all," she snarled and regained control of the chains. "We need to get out of here now." She took hold of Berith's arm, and they stepped in time, through the frigid wards. They'd just made it through the barrier when a screech captured her attention.

She released Berith. "Get her out of here," she ordered.

"Like hell," he answered, and for a moment, she saw a glimmer of the demon who'd once captured her heart.

She'd slid the knife back into her boot before they'd left the cavern, so now, her hand moved to the hilt of her sword. It warmed beneath her touch as the cavern was filled by gyrating demons, large and small.

Her gaze narrowed, sizing up her first opponent. She lifted her sword, and as it came toward her, nails scratching and teeth dripping with saliva, it swung and sliced. Blood spattered, but she moved forward, intent on the protection of the group.

Dagda slid beside her. "Brings back old times, yeah?"

"Indeed," she muttered as another demon launched at her.

Her arm swung as another dropped before her, and a quick glance told her that the legion filled the tunnel.

Slice, step, slide, swing became the mantra she fought by. Dagda chuckled with each kill, but it felt never-ending. Sweat slid down her back as the clash of steel on bone echoed loudly. Screeching topped off the cacophony along with cries of pain.

A creature landed on her shoulder and bit deep. Before she could grab it though, it was wrenched away, and the ripe, coppery scent of blood filled her senses and drove her harder. But every swing sapped her energy.

"Keep going, Danu," chanted Morrigan on her left, and she nodded.

"We'll fight them off yet," she answered, but the strain was telling in her voice.

A hand slid around her waist, and before she could argue, her knees sagged, and her energy fled.

She was pulled from the front line of the battle, and glancing up, she noted it was Berith, a tiny dribble of blood sliding down his temples. She fought against his hold, but it was little more than a cursory "put me down," because she knew her flagging energy would be a hindrance now.

Moments passed before Dagda, Morrigan, and even Lugh pulled back. "We've done what we can, but retreat would be best now," Morrigan muttered.

Zazrael whimpered as Berith slid the chain free from the ring where he'd secured him. "Let me go," he pleaded, but Berith merely grunted.

It was Morrigan who took the chains. "Return us to the meadow," she demanded.

Zazrael nodded as they formed up and used his magic to return to where they'd massed. Once there, Macha stepped forward. She swung her long, red hair over her shoulder and scanned those assembled. "We canna let him go, Dagda, but he may yet have some use."

Berith settled Danu on her feet, and she tugged away from him, weak but intending to stand alone, just as she always had.

"Aye," Dagda muttered in response to Macha's comment.

"Morrigan, release him to me. I'll be his gatekeeper," Macha stated, and while Danu watched, the other goddess handed the chains over.

"He must not return to Marrer," Morrigan growled. All those gathered nodded their agreement.

"Oh, he won't," Macha said, her smile cold and more than a little feral. "If he even thinks it, his regrets will never end." Then she and her prisoner were gone from sight.

Danu slid down to the log, watching in silence as the group drifted away until only Dagda, Morrigan, and Berith remained with her.

"You should go home and heal," Morrigan said, her gaze steely.

"Aye, but has she the power left?" queried Dagda, squatting before her. "Danu, can you make it?"

Unable to speak, Danu simply nodded, though honestly, that might be the end of her power. At least until she had time to regroup and recharge a little.

"I'll take her," muttered Berith.

Dagda cast a piercing frown at Berith. "Ye've done enough, Berith."

Morrigan crowded in. "You should be grateful that she'll even assist you…"

Danu cleared her throat and shook her head. "It's fine, brethren. He'll return me to my home, then leave." Heaven knew that now wasn't the time for anyone to say something she'd regret. Like he'd given her a promise all the years ago and promptly forgot it.

She stood, tottered in the slight breeze. "Take me home, Berith. Please?"

He took her hand, and everything melted away.

Berith held her close, letting her essence settle the sudden clamour of fury that was slowly infusing him.

She'd come at his call, she'd trusted him in her home, yet there was something more. It was at the very edge of his consciousness, poking and prodding for him to remember. *Why can't I?*

She wavered on her feet in her kitchen, the room warm but dark, with only a candle lighting the gloom. "Naamah must have retired," she muttered. "I'm going to clean up then do the same."

The words were a dismissal. He shook his head. "No, you need help. Let me."

Her face was white, and he didn't miss the flash of something in her eyes.

He cupped her cheek. "Let me help you," he said, keeping the words soft. Whisps of her long, strawberry blonde hair had escaped its bindings, and the shadows beneath her eyes betrayed her exhaustion. "I can tend your wounds," he offered.

"You should go," she said, her voice unsteady, and looked away.

"What did I do?" The words burst out of him.

She slumped, and he saw the sudden sheen of tears and the wobble of her lips. It was as if the steel of her spine had fled, leaving her defenceless. It clawed at his guts.

"Danu? What did I do?"

Now when she turned back to look at him, such sorrow as he'd never before seen on her face froze the marrow in his bones. "You left me, Berith." She bit her lip, before she gasped and cupped a hand over her mouth.

"When? When did I leave you?" Something was building, his chest was tight, like a band stopped him from breathing. "When?"

"After you promised me everything!" Her eyes were pools of misery. "You told me you loved me! You said you'd be by my side for eternity, then you left me for Marrer's bed! How could you do that to me? You said you loved me, Berith. You made me your promise!"

She slid down into a puddle at his feet, and he stared at her. Horror dawning. "I…" He couldn't continue the thought. Memory surged forward, smashing through the dam which had contained it and all the memories. "I…"

He watched, stunned and frozen, as she struggled back to her feet and retreated from him, so she was little more than a wraith in the darkness. "Go. Leave me alone, Berith."

She moved slowly, like an old woman, toward the bedroom. His feet moved, shadowing her. Needing to know more… All!

Marrer. The bitch, she'd somehow cast a spell over him. One that made him forget.

10

Danu staggered to her bed and dropped, uncaring that she was filthy and covered with blood and grime. She undid the belt with scabbard and sword and slid it under the bed. She'd deal with it in the morning; right now, she just couldn't cope. Nothing much mattered because he'd smashed through her cloak of dignity. The only thing that kept her pain and loss inside her.

Tears burned her cheeks, but she didn't swipe them away. That would take more energy than she had, and she felt heavy, limbs like lead.

It wasn't until Berith's hand touched her shoulder that she realised he hadn't gone. She jumped and glanced up at him through the veil of moisture.

"I'm sorry, Danu," he muttered, sounding so sad.

It just made her cry harder, because him pitying her wasn't what she desired. "Please, just leave me, Berith," she sobbed.

"I can't, Danu. I left you once before."

His words opened some door within her, urging her to release the fury she'd banked for years. The agony she'd suppressed. Heat licked at her insides, and she surged up. "Don't you dare. Don't you soothe me with your pity. I may have been weak before, but that's not an excuse for you to pretend."

"I'm not," he sputtered.

But she was lost, the haze of release overshadowing her ability to think clearly. It spewed out of her, a raging torrent of suffering. "I loved you. You are the only one who ever understood me, held me. Loved me. I gave you everything and you stomped on it and me! How could you do that? Then you went to Marrer. Somehow you broke your promise and pledged yourself to her, and I was alone again. The sun went dark that day. You shattered me, Berith!"

His hands slid around her, tugged her close as she shuddered. Her broken core exposed to him, and she clutched him close, because he was the only anchor in the sea of loss buffeted her.

"I'm so sorry, Danu. I don't know what happened or how. I didn't mean to leave you."

"But... you... did." She closed her eyes, wanting the pain to end. Wanting it to be done, because this affliction was too much for even a goddess to bear. For all the magic she'd had, she was bereft.

"I'm here now," he muttered, sounding almost as ragged as she felt.

Heaven help her, she needed him to hold her. To soothe the edges that were raw, but even as she tried to pull away, he kept her against him, and she wondered if he was trying to absorb the maelstrom inside her. "It's not enough," she hiccupped, making every effort to pull herself together.

"Don't..." he gulped. "Stay there, still. Please."

She stilled in his arms. "Berith? Will you..." She swallowed. "I know you don't love me, but kiss me? Please? One last time." Because this would be the last time. Once this was done, she was ready to let go.

"Don't say that."

She sighed and now pulled back. Her hand rose, and with a snap of her fingers the candles around the bed lit. "I do, Berith. Once this is done, I'm leaving."

"No. I won't let you." His eyes were red, and his face drawn.

"You can't stop me. This is my choice and my right."

He shook his head. "I made mistakes, Danu. I let you go, and I know I should have held tighter, but I won't let you fade."

"And what would you know about that?" she asked. When he shifted, a seed of understanding planted itself in her mind. "You know my plans. How?"

He shrugged, pushing his hands into the pockets of his pants. "I just know. You're necessary to this world. To your brethren. To…" He swallowed, and she watched the bob of his Adam's apple. "To me."

"I don't do pity."

"There's no fucking pity," he snarled. "You mean a lot to me. I don't quite understand how much…"

"Get out," she screamed because she couldn't handle any more emotional dithering.

He snatched at her, his face tight. Dragging her close, she was on tiptoes when their mouths smashed together in a brutal kiss. His lips demanded entry, and she couldn't deny him. When his tongue slid against hers, she was lost, fingers sliding up to his shoulders and biting in as she clutched him. Needing him. Needing the sighs and even the lies if that's what it took.

The kiss moved, and somehow it was against her jaw. She arched, desperate for his touch. "Berith," she whispered, and his groan fed her soul.

Her fingers slid down, found the closures of his jacket.

"Keep going," he demanded, tongue sliding against her throat in a way she'd always loved.

She shook as she tore his jacket and shirt open, and finally, hot flesh was revealed. She slid the pads of her fingertips down its muscular length. Her touch reminding her of the dips and hollows she'd not seen for hundreds of years.

Heat suffused her again; this the fire of carnal hunger, and she shivered as her body readied itself for the connection to him, one she'd denied herself for so long. No one else had ever made her feel as he did. She'd never sought another lover, because it was Berith…

A tiny sliver of magic moved in the air, and she was naked against him. "Oh please," she muttered, hoping he'd understand what she pleaded for.

"Let me love you tonight," he whispered as his lips hovered over her collarbone.

She nodded her acceptance, and then the second had passed as she danced in the light and joy of anticipation. Her breasts ached, and the place between her legs throbbed... urging her to demand more.

The slide of his skin against hers was electric. Her nipples were tight buds, and when his skin touched her, she sucked in an unsteady breath. "I don't know that I can wait," she muttered and stepped to the bed, slid down and waited for him to join her.

She was aflame and so ready, her core melting as her body responded to the stimuli.

"I want you, but I don't know if I can hold out long enough to bring you pleasure," he gritted, advancing slowly as his cock wavered before her gaze.

"Come to me now," she demanded, and he sighed, climbing onto the bed and covering her, framing her face with his arms. "Please?"

His chest was moving in and out as he dropped his forehead against hers. "I want to give you pleasure."

"You are pleasure. Fill me, please. I can't wait any longer." And she couldn't. Instead of waiting for him to move, she lifted her legs, slid them around his waist. "No longer will I be a mere vessel," she muttered and flexed, felt the probing of his length and impaled herself. "I will take what I desire most of all," she promised.

She arched as she welcomed him deep, heard his groan as she moved, hips gyrating and demanding, and he was there, moving with her. Taking and giving. Filling her up until there was no more space. She closed her eyes, banking every feeling, every sound and scent in her mind, so it would fill her for eternity. Then she splintered, welcoming the orgasm that crashed down over her.

"I love you, Danu. I always did." He thrust hard and she felt him release deep inside her.

Tears seeped, because it was beautiful and yet signalled that once dawn came, he'd leave her again. He held her tight as their bodies cooled and the racing of the beating hearts settled.

"I... Did I hurt you?" he asked, his voice cracking.

She opened her eyes. "No." She cupped his face and made herself smile. And even if he had... She couldn't hurt him, because that would be like shoving a knife into her heart. "You didn't hurt me."

Berith lay still, holding naked Danu close against his side as she sighed in her sleep. It was torture. The intimacy had been... unforgettable. The knowledge that he'd hurt her so badly, insupportable.

How? How did this happen?

He'd never understood her coldness, not until now. The truth was he'd been blind to how she felt and that he couldn't forgive himself for that.

The silence of her house soothed him, and for a moment, he wished this could be his future, but he couldn't plan anything like that until she trusted him and he resolved the situation with Marrer.

Danu snuffled in her sleep, turning to him in a way he could only dream of.

He'd told her he loved her. "It wasn't a lie," he said.

But what could he offer her? Not much right now. He was bound to Marrer, and he couldn't offer Danu anything else until he'd rectified that, but the knowledge that she planned her fade was terrifying.

"I will keep her safe," he promised, but knowing how hadn't yet emerged. He closed his eyes and let himself rest.

The bed was warm and comfortable, though her body ached, Danu thought, rising through the layers of sleep. Why...? Memories came, flooding into her, and she slid her hand along the sheet and was unsurprised to find it empty.

She bit her lip, hard. Felt the burst and tang of copper, as she kept the tears at bay.

He'd left.

Opening her eyes was something she dreaded, but she forced them to move anyway. Light was spilling over the room, the watery sunrise telling her the time of pleasure had been and gone, and she made herself rise.

"You're up already." His voice came from the doorway, and she spun.

Surprise and joy filled her. "You stayed," she breathed.

"I'm not leaving you again, Danu." He entered the room and placed two cups on the small table. "I made tea."

She laughed, the sound wet and snotty. "I…"

"I'm sorry I hurt you, Danu. I still don't know what happened or how, but I will find out. I'll never be able to regain the time lost, but never again." His slow steps toward her reinforced the gravity of his words.

"And Marrer?"

He shook his head. "I don't know how it happened, but the time has come for me to call Lord Lucifer. To seek his guidance."

Danu blinked. "I know where he is," she whispered.

Now it was his turn to appear surprised. "You do?"

She nodded. "He's… We meet sometimes. He knew how hurt I was, not that he ever said anything. But he's kept tabs on the situation with Marrer."

"He knows what she did?"

Danu shrugged. "I don't know exactly how much or if he's aware of the details, though knowing him, it's likely. I never asked and he never offered. It didn't seem right. You have free will, and neither of us, I guess, had any intention of impeding it." There'd been countless times she'd wished she could, but it seemed wrong, so she made a point of never asking.

"I need to see him."

She reached out a shaking hand. "But not today. We need to meet with the others… Have Luke and Grace arrived yet?"

He quirked a brow. "And you're well-informed."

"I'm a goddess, it's what I do. Along with my natural roles." Her smile was small, but she felt the muscles in her face tighten as she answered.

He tugged her into his embrace. "You never took another mate."

She'd declared her love during their passionate encounter last night, but explaining would expose more of her secrets. And protecting herself had become second nature in the last centuries.

"I… When one like me makes a declaration, it's difficult to be with another," she said. "There are ramifications for me and the other. It's not impossible, but sacrifices are required, and I… I couldn't be with someone else, unless there was love." She shrugged. She had no intention of telling him that the sacrifice involved something he held dear. That Balala had offered herself once she'd realised the depths of Danu's love for Berith.

"Yes, Luke and Grace arrived yesterday," he said, answering her previous question. "In all the madness, I didn't have an opportunity to tell you."

She nodded. "We should meet with them. Then, perhaps it's time to regroup, consider what we know and how to go forward."

He stopped her before she could dress. "Wait," he murmured and leaned in to kiss her. "You should drink your tea first. It's early."

She smiled. "My days are usually starting early. Ask…" She frowned. "Where is Naamah?"

He sighed. "She was up and muttered something about post-partum Zelda?"

"Ah, yes. I've been teaching her so she can assist…" Her words died away, and she glanced toward the window, hoping he wouldn't read the truth in her eyes.

"When you fade and she's in Brigid's service?"

Shock speared her and she turned. "How do you know?"

"Naamah found your plans. She's… She brought them to me."

Ice settled in Danu's gut. "That's why this elaborate…" Her hand flung out while fury, horror, and something even more insidious whispered she'd been a pity fuck again. She stood. "Leave me," she whispered.

His face flamed. "What?"

"I don't need your pity," she said. "I'll assist you in the battle for—"

"Don't be a fucking imbecile, Danu. If you think I'm going anywhere, you're sorely mistaken. If you've some misguided notion that I made love to you because of that list, forget it. I thought you knew me better." Exasperation threaded through his words.

"I thought I did. Once, long ago, I would have said so." Her lips were tight, and she spoke slowly. The words were almost impossible to say.

He reached for her, hauled her close. "I've made a fucking mess of all of this, but you and me? I will give you honest and demand the same from you. No more keeping secrets, love."

She laughed. "That's a bit rich…"

"Yes, yes, it is. But I'm not the kind of demon who can't and doesn't learn. I lost you, and this, and I made you pay. But no more, Danu. You and I, we're fated. I know it."

She closed her eyes, leaned in, needing his heat and strength. "I don't know how to trust you," she whispered.

"I know, love. I know."

11

The two couples waited by the door, and Danu fidgeted with her hair, while Berith gripped her hand in his. "It's fine."

"They only know me as Danu, the goddess. I'm… This is difficult for me," she whispered.

He knew over the centuries she'd taken great care to project a cold façade. It made him ache, knowing he'd been the cause. And while she presented herself in a dark blue dress, which moulded against her trim figure, it was her own visage today. Her hair was a shining mass, sliding down over her shoulders, her red hair a foil for her emerald-green eyes and lush, strawberry-coloured lips.

He too assumed his base form, a demon with black skin, red claws, and shining ruby eyes. He wondered for the first time, should she wish to procreate, what any child of theirs might look like? Would it have her fine, pale skin or his black and leathery hide? He'd seen many demi-demons, like Grace and Naamah. Even Fenella was human-looking. He'd need to consult the many tomes of the library once this situation was finally resolved.

"Come on in," called Fenella, opening the door wide to admit them both.

They entered the house, and Danu extended her hand first to

Fenella then Padraic. "Thank you for opening your home for this meeting," she murmured and smiled at Padraic. "Well, Lord of Leprechauns, it's nice to step foot inside this house once more."

Berith frowned. "Again?"

Danu smiled, her lips curving upward. "I've delivered generations of the family here, the last was… Fenella. Not that you'd remember me. However, on the top floor, there was a hidden key, yes?"

Fenella's eyes widened. "Yes, there was."

"Yes, times have moved on. Now, introduce me to Grace and Luke, please." Her smile was soft.

The younger couple stepped forward, and Berith introduced Luke. "He's a lycan. From Australia."

"I've never been there, but I'm told it's warmer than here. I think, one day, I might like to visit," Danu said.

"It's lovely, there's nowhere like it on earth. Uh, I'm Grace," the woman said.

"Indeed. I see some of Vinta in you too. He's a faithful servant to Berith." Danu took her hand with a smile. "Ah, and you shall be richly rewarded in about eight months."

Grace appeared startled. "What?"

Berith frowned. "Uh, could we perhaps settle into business now, then…"

Fenella smiled. "Come this way, we have a meeting room set up through here."

The group followed her into a room where a long table had been set up with a carafe of coffee and a collection of finger foods. Danu settled herself at the table and Berith took a seat beside her. He didn't miss the slight grin she cast in his direction.

"Thank you, Fenella and Padraic," Berith said. "We have discovered one of the sources of Marrer's magic. The goddess Ate was rescued yesterday. It's going to cause a hit to Marrer's supply, so the sooner we can move against her, the better."

Padraic cleared his throat. "This would be easier with more assistance."

"Other pantheons will not grant assistance, as they have no

interest in getting into an argument they are not involved in. Perhaps you could reach out to your varied contacts?"

Padraic sighed. "We've already begun that process, however, the grounds aren't yet ready." He frowned. "And the fairies who control the land are unwilling to allow us to use it until we can assure them of their safety."

Berith rubbed his brow. "What?"

"If I may?" Fenella spoke softly. "When I was abducted, they helped, but it also reminded them that they are among the weaker members of our alliance. They want an undertaking that we will protect them. Padraic can promise, but they need to know the pantheon and the demons will protect them, their lands, and most importantly, their forests."

"I'm willing to talk to my brethren," Danu offered.

"I can give an undertaking for me and mine, but more than that would need to come from Lucifer," Berith growled, because while he might be reasonably assured Lucifer would grant such an undertaking, it wasn't his place to offer it. *I need to talk to him. Soon.*

"I suggest we reconvene back here in a few days, if that suits everyone?" Padraic offered, and those gathered around the table unanimously agreed to that plan.

Marrer prowled the cavern. "How could this happen?" she raged.

Zazrael was an idiot, and as far as she could see, the only thing he had in his favour was that she... *she* was his sister.

"You're sure that Zazrael was in Berith's clutches?"

The demon shook before her. "Yes, Lady Marrer. Berith brought a contingent, including the members of the Celtic pantheon, into your private cavern with the intent of finding your prisoner. The guards you'd set there attempted to protect your holdings, but Zazrael..." His wing tips drooped as he dropped his head. "He took them through the wards. They took the goddess Ate from the facility, Lady."

"How?"

"You granted him blood rights, Lady. They had hold of him."

"Who had hold of him? You said *they*." Marrer leaned closer, but the demon danced back, just slightly out of range, and damn Berith, but her magic levels had dropped significantly. That alone had told her that something had occurred.

"The Goddess Danu, Lady," the demon husked.

"Danu?" Marrer pulled herself up onto her bloated legs and advanced. For each step she took, advancing, the demon scuttled back further and faster.

"Yes, Lady."

Fury whipped through her, and she felt the pressure in her guts and head. "That bitch! That redheaded whore! I will strip her entrails from her body and strangle her with them. Then when I get done with Danu, I'll make Berith pay." She spat fire in the direction of the demon, who cowered against the wall.

She reached into the bowl sitting on the stand, lifted the bloodied flesh, and slid it into her mouth, licking her lips to ensure none of the magically infused blood was lost.

"Get me more flesh, I don't care how or where. Go!" she thundered, and the minion hurried out of the room.

"I will destroy them. Both of them, but I need more power." She stalked back to her throne and slumped down, closing her eyes as the trickle of magic slid through her limbs. "I'll make my plans tomorrow," she whispered. "Tomorrow.

Danu entered her house, aware that Berith followed her in. It wasn't embarrassing really, or so she told herself. If Naamah had worked out that they'd slept together, she hadn't said anything, but Danu was well aware that the demon watched them enter with a small smile on her lips.

"Should I put the kettle on, Danu?" Naamah queried.

She nodded, and they settled into the seats in the kitchen as Naamah bustled around.

"Do you think we'll be ready soon?" Danu asked.

Berith shrugged. "I hope so."

As Naamah was setting the cups before them, a flaming envelope appeared on her table. "Well, that was quicker than I expected," she said drily.

Berith snatched it up. "Who? And what?"

"Zeus," she answered, picking the letter from his hand and blowing on it to extinguish the flame. She opened the missive and winced. "We've been summoned," she muttered. "I hate when he does this."

"When?"

She sighed. "When we finish our coffee, I'm thinking. Have you ever met him before?"

Berith shook his head. "Why would…"

"He's Ate's father, so my guess is this meeting will be of the 'why she's been missing' and 'how come we found her' variety."

"Huh, so he's not very involved with his offspring," Berith said.

She giggled. "No, but to be fair, both the Greek and Roman pantheons are similar in outlook."

They sipped their coffee, and she considered Berith from beneath her lowered lids. In either form, he was perfect for her. If only he understood. She sighed inwardly. Would this last? She'd been avoiding the question since he'd basically re-entered her life. He wasn't making any grand promises, and right now, she was too scared to ask him to.

They finished in silence, then she stood. "You'll need to hold my hand—their security is much tighter than mine." She lifted the summons and used it to transfer them to Zeus' waiting room.

His secretary was waiting with a smile. "Danu, so good to see you again, and you brought a… friend." Her eyes were the only things that betrayed her surprise at Berith's appearance.

Danu smiled, because she really wasn't sure how else to explain the situation.

The door cracked open, and the secretary sighed. "I guess he's ready to see you," she muttered before indicating that they both should enter into the chamber beyond.

Danu sauntered in, aware that Berith hovered behind her. "Hello, Zeus. It's been a very long time."

The god seated at the long office desk raised his brow. "Has it?"

"At least twenty years," she replied with a shrug. "So, you called for me?"

"I hear you were involved in freeing my daughter, Ate?"

"We both were," Danu said, gesturing to Berith.

"You brought a demon with you?" Zeus said.

"Yes," she answered through gritted teeth. "But that's not why I'm here, so let's get down to the business, shall we?" Danu made a show of taking the seat and waited for Berith to settle beside her.

"What happened to Ate? She's refusing my summons, and I want to know," he said, reclining in his chair.

"Well, it seems a demon, Marrer, captured her. She was planning her fade," Danu said and watched as Zeus winced.

"She has always been highly strung," he replied.

"She was being used as a battery for holding magic, then bled almost dry. Marrer's brother, Zazrael, was her jailer. We merely found out who and where and went in to remove her."

Danu wasn't interested in getting into the middle of their family dispute. *They always end badly.* Especially when Zeus was involved, she thought and had to contain a snort.

"You find me funny, Danu? I cannot say I understand you. I have many children, and it's my right and—"

Berith cleared his throat, stopping Zeus' commentary. "Danu simply came to tell you about Ate. She is recovering, though it will be protracted," he explained.

Danu couldn't stop the smile. "Indeed, it was Berith who was able to find out from Zazrael where she was being held. It appears that Marrer understood Ate's magic was already waning, and she—Marrer—could offer her unlimited power, and Ate believed her. Not that it was a lie, but Ate was gullible. It was a last chance to gain your attention and didn't work."

Zeus rose up, brow furrowed. "Beware, Danu. You know that angering me is unwise."

She plastered a polite smile on her face. "I will let Ate know to contact you once she feels suitably recovered and able."

Zeus opened his mouth, but Danu had enough of playing sweet, so she rose and took Berith's hand.

"You also know my anger is legendary," she said, "I have learned restraint, but to be honest, Zeus, you're so officious and I honestly don't know how blind you can be. So, here's my last word on it. Ate tried to gain your attention and good will for many years. You were a remote father, only interested in what your children can do for you, and as a result she felt she'd failed and was prepared to step away. Maybe…" She inhaled, letting her ire settle a little. "Maybe you should think on the reasons she was prepared to take this decision and what you, as her father, can do for her."

Tugging on Berith's hand, she turned.

"Danu?" Zeus called to her. She glanced over her shoulder and noted that the cold façade he wore had melted away. "I… Thank you."

She nodded, and they left the room together. Once in the anteroom, she stopped by the secretary's desk. "He may need a few minutes," she said to the woman hovering outside.

Berith's hand flexed in hers. "You did well to hold onto your temper," he told her as they once more entered her kitchen.

12

Berith didn't want to leave, but his own work, the care of the great library, was calling. Hauling Danu close, he whispered, "I have to go."

She didn't stiffen or pull away, and it made him acutely aware of how much damage his blindness of her needs, and the sacrifices she'd made, had done to them. He hated it.

"Come with me," he offered.

Shaking her head, Danu stepped away with a smile. "I can't. I've left my responsibilities to Naamah for long enough. She's neither trained nor has the power to ensure safe deliveries. But I do understand." Her hand rose to his cheek. "Thank you," she whispered, and he knew it was a dismissal. Kind and soft, but nonetheless, she was telling him to go.

Long seconds passed as pain slid its icy fingers along his spine. "I'll be back," he promised.

She remained silent, looking at him. He couldn't read the expression on her face, and he realised he rarely could these days. She'd schooled herself well against any and all eventualities, and she was protecting her heart. He couldn't blame her, but then again, he wanted to heal it and didn't know where to start.

Finally, he turned away, even though the pain radiated, and stepped through the fold of space and into his library.

Vinta waited, his face tight. "Come. See."

Berith growled. "What's wrong now, Vinta?"

The demon sighed, grabbed his hand. "Come. See." He tugged Berith toward the far wall, where a tiny hourglass sat. He'd noted it there so many times, but what could be special about it? It was just an hourglass… wasn't it?

In the dimness, at the far end of the room, it sparkled. "And?" he demanded of Vinta.

"Magic," wheezed Vinta. "Not. Here."

Berith shook his head. "It's here, how can it not be here?"

Vinta was muttering riddles, and he really wasn't in the mood. He had to find where the missing page may have gone and what its importance was.

"No. From. Else." Vinta gestured to the glass again, and Berith frowned.

"From somewhere else?" he guessed, and Vinta nodded his head. "And this is important?"

Vinta nodded again. "Look. See."

He glanced at it. As he did so, the lighting in the library dimmed a little. "What was that?" Berith muttered, then ignored it, instead inspecting the item, noting it was old, the metal tarnished and covered in dust.

Berith felt a prickle of magic as he picked it up and brushed some of the dust away. Motes danced in the air, and Vinta sneezed. A symbol appeared, and Berith grunted; three interwoven circlets or spirals.

"I've seen this before," Berith murmured. *But where?* "We need to get to work, Vinta," he ordered and placed the item down, feeling the loss of power.

Shrugging it off, he started to run through the list of what he planned to accomplish.

"Come, Vinta. Today we'll look for the resource titles. They may have a clue to the missing page." He noted Vinta seemed uncomfortable leaving the darkened end of the library. "Come now," he urged, and they began once more searching for the knowledge of the missing page.

Danu's body ached as she stretched her back.

"Danu?" queried Naamah, waiting beside her.

"A long day," she answered. "The delivery was difficult, transverse. I nearly lost them both, but finally, we prevailed."

After each difficult birth, she longed to do nothing more than rest her weary body in a bath of warm water, but she had to refill the well first. The magic well was something she'd been doing for a long time, ever since Marrer... Her mind shied away from the knowledge of the demon and the risk she'd been taking for so long. She placed her hand against the symbol on the wall and allowed herself to drift enough, while the punch of magic which had infused her drained away to lower and more manageable levels.

By the time she was done, she could only stagger to her room. "I'll bathe first. Leave the meal, we can arrange it once I return," she whispered, and as her door closed, she began divesting herself of her bloodied gown.

The water was ready, not quite steaming, but hot enough to relax muscles. Every inch of her body had taken a battering with the turning of the child. While the mother had relaxed once Danu had arrived, she'd set to work, carefully and laboriously ensuring the babe transitioned into the best possible delivery position before finally bringing the child into the world.

She closed her eyes and let her satisfaction fill her, and rested until she felt ready to rise and face the mess that awaited her.

The secrets she still kept battered her mind. Memories of the night she'd passed with Berith two days ago were difficult to ignore. Though he'd told her he loved her, he was still bound body and flesh to Marrer. Until he found a way to address that, there could be no future for them.

"And I can't allow myself to dwell on that." No, she still had her plan, but there were things to do first. Marrer and Zazrael and their minions to defeat, then she'd need to settle her affairs.

One beautiful night of ultimate pleasure couldn't overcome centuries of pain and loss.

She rose, grabbed the towel, and felt pleased that her muscles no longer ached. "Time to eat," she told herself as her stomach growled.

Once Danu was dressed, she returned to the kitchen as Naamah paced. "Finally. I feel like I could eat the head off a wild boar," muttered Naamah.

"Sorry, I just needed to wash the day away," she answered.

"What was that you were doing, with the wall?" queried Naamah. "It looked intense."

Without thinking, she answered. "The library needs to be reinforced. I promised Lucifer years ago that I would continue to do so."

A growl echoed behind her, and ice trickled through her veins as she turned.

"Lucifer asked you to reinforce the library?" Berith advanced, his eyes flashing scarlet. He might be in human form, but there was no denying either the power or the rage emanating from him.

Naamah muttered something and hurried from the room, while Danu considered the best way to soothe the currently furious demon before her. "I... I promised him a long time ago, any extra power I would push toward the wards. He knew Marrer was determined to..."

"You've been reinforcing the wards since when?" She couldn't ignore the fury in Berith's query.

"Since Marrer appeared as your consort," she whispered, holding herself up to her full height. "He... He knew things would get worse, and he needed you to concentrate on your task."

His lips twisted. "You didn't tell me?"

She gulped, because how did you explain keeping something like that a secret? She refused to blame Lucifer, because he'd given her a choice, one she'd accepted.

She sighed. "You should sit down, Berith. I'll explain what I can, but some things... They aren't really my secrets." And since her kind were keepers of secrets... After all, wasn't that why the Tuatha had been ejected from their homeworld? She watched as he complied, every movement a jerk which had her nerves jumping.

"Tell. Me."

She settled opposite him. "I am, or was, a powerful goddess. One who gave my heart, freely. But the one I loved, the one who was the other half of me, never saw it. But Lucifer did. He knew... One day, after Marrer, and before he left, he came and asked me how I felt. When we take a life partner, it's that...for life. The Dagda and Morrigan and the others? They all found their partners, and while we have no ceremony or physical ceremony, we can give one-sided if that's the way our luck runs." She shrugged, because she was baring a part of herself that she'd protected, hidden, for centuries. "We are keepers of secrets, so my agreement with Lucifer was just that, a secret. One that had to remain hidden until something happened," she mumbled.

"Why?" His question was raw.

She blinked. "Why?"

"Why, when your magic is fading, would you do that? Give up what little you have."

Danu bit her lip and dropped her head, thinking about the question. The easy answer was because Lucifer requested it. But Berith deserved more than a glib and easy answer.

"Because I wanted you safe," she whispered. "Marrer is dangerous. I saw that early on, as did Lucifer. It's part of the reason why he left. He needed you to find yourself, the truth, and to become what you could be."

She glanced up to see him blinking, face slack. "What the hell does that mean?"

"You have a future, one more than simply the librarian, and Lucifer saw that in you. But he couldn't tell you, and neither could I."

"Marrer...?"

"Oh, for heaven's sake," she muttered. "She's not the key to your future or your past. She's simply a power-hungry bitch," she shrieked. *When will he finally get the message?*

Pushing away from the table, she shoved the chair back so hard it bounced off the tabletop and toward her. Before it made contact, it stilled, and magic, old and steeped in the ancient ways, flickered through the air.

Another being, clothed in red, appeared and loped toward her.

It bowed low, and she returned the action. "Lord Lucifer, it has been an age," she growled.

He thrust back his hood. "It's good to see you, Danu. You're a bit pale and wan-looking, but I guess the years take their toll, huh?" When he turned, she watched Berith's lips flatten.

"My lord."

Lucifer snorted, "After all these years, you still use the formal addresses? Come, Berith, it's your brother-in-arms. Lucifer. Say my name for once."

Berith snarled, "My lord… *Lucifer*."

Lucifer snorted with mirth. "He doesn't change much, does he?" he said, and winked at Danu who didn't contain her smile.

"Only a very little, friend." She dragged out a chair. "It's been a long time, so come, sit and I'll arrange some food. Naamah?" she called.

The demon entered the room, squeaked on seeing Lucifer, and fell to the floor. "My great lord," she whispered.

"Naamah, I'm glad you're finally here, where you belong. But I regret the loss of your sibling."

Naamah's head bobbed up and down, though she remained on the floor, eyes averted.

"Come, let's prepare some food," said Danu, stooping down to help the prostrate demon rise. "Lucifer enjoys upsetting people, but it's all good-natured. Well, usually."

Lucifer guffawed. "Ah, sit down, ladies, and allow me." With a clap of his hands, a feast appeared on the table. Game and vegetables. Fruits and steaming pies. A flacon of wine and four goblets. "We shall drink and eat and be merry, before we discuss the situation before us."

13

It wasn't that Lucifer appeared just as he was ready to explode, Berith told himself. It certainly wasn't because he realised the depths of what Danu had done and was continuing to do… even the sacrifices she continued to make that left him incandescent with rage. It was that she kept it a secret after what they'd shared recently. It felt as if she'd somehow wounded him mortally.

Except he was a demon, was he even supposed to feel this way? Hurt and frustration only scratched the surface of his roiling emotions.

After the meal, the women rose to clear the table while Lucifer watched him. It was uncomfortable. "What?" he asked.

"Have you felt it yet? That you're changing?" Lucifer queried.

More confusion filled Berith. "You're talking in circles," he muttered.

"And you're ignoring my question. We'll discuss it later on then, when you're ready to hear what I have to say, but for now, tell me what you know. What you need to know, and I'll assist as and where I can. But beware, I'm limited in what I can share. We're all bound by conventions and rules in this fight. Even as Lord of the Underworld, there is only so much I can tell you." Lucifer leaned back in his seat, a slight smile on his lips.

Berith glared at the creature sitting opposite him, and when Naamah laid her hand on his shoulder, he nearly jumped. "I will retire, my lords." She bowed deeply, turned to Danu. "If you have no further need of me, that is?" When Danu shook her head, Naamah removed herself from the room while Danu took her seat at the table.

"So, what did I miss?" Danu asked.

Berith glanced at her, noting the pinched edges of her lips, and grimaced. Once more he was causing her worry.

Lucifer looked back at him then to Danu. "Well, I think, first and foremost, you are needing to hear about Danu's actions, and why she's doing it."

"I suppose that's a start," snarled Berith, staring at Danu, who rubbed at the frown lines between her eyes.

"Alright." She steepled her hands, and he had the distinct impression she was preparing herself for his explosion. "I made an agreement with Lucifer, after Balala died and around the time you entered into your relationship with Marrer. You know many things are foreknown, because many are written in your library, but this was something that Lucifer knew of. I don't know exactly what Lucifer does, but he said the library had to be protected. That any extra power would be necessary to affect this. So, I sent an item—"

"The hourglass," he muttered, and she nodded.

"It was small, inconspicuous. You weren't likely to note it, and to be honest, clearly after so long, you took it for granted." She shrugged.

It enraged him. "You bled yourself of magic."

"Only the excess. Only that which was drawn from my work, not my own essential magic."

He waited, expecting her to somehow argue her decision, his fingers clenched with expectation of something he didn't want to hear, and when she didn't, he glared at Lucifer. "You used her."

"No. She is a creature of free will. As are you." Lucifer smiled at him sadly. "So was Balala, and so is Marrer. Free will cannot be curtailed or foresworn. You know that. What she did was done for love, Berith."

He snarled and shoved away from the table. "Riddles. My life is lived in riddles."

She must have stood, because she was there, her soft hand on his shoulder. "I make my own choices." The words she didn't say hung in the air.

Closing his eyes didn't change the facts. Knowing she was fading, she still siphoned power into his library shield. Weakened herself for him. He'd been blind to so many things. "You need to stop it," he whispered.

"You need me to do this, Berith."

"No, I… I need you." He reached blindly for her hands.

"I think it's time to let the shields drop," Lucifer said, his voice cutting through the private moment.

Berith spun, tugging Danu with him so she was nestled against his chest. "What?"

"What she wants is no longer there," Lucifer said, his eyes narrowed. "But before we let the shields down, get your minions out of there. Vinta in particular."

"Vinta?" He wasn't sure exactly what Lucifer was hedging around, so he waited. If his lord had something in particular to impart, he'd do so. *In his own time, of course*, thought Berith sourly.

Lucifer nodded. "Vinta is important, not just to you, but to our aim."

"He can't come here, but my temple has lodgings. It's protected," Danu muttered.

"Good. When I leave, move them with speed. Now, before I go, there's one other thing that I must tell you." Lucifer indicated everyone should sit down again, and with a boulder settled in his belly, Berith followed the directive.

"Balala knew the truth. I told her what I knew before she died. She also knew your child was unable to survive." Lucifer shook his head. "She, as with all of us, had a part to play, Berith. As did the child."

He felt the familiar grief, though it was muted, like a faded memory. "What do you need me to know?"

"She began your transformation, or evolution, more correctly."

Berith shook his head again, unwilling to continue this nonsense of half-truths and only enough information to confuse and frustrate.

Before he could open his mouth to remonstrate, Lucifer continued. "You were never meant to remain static, you had a part to play, as did Balala and… Danu."

Fear clutched him. "Danu?"

Lucifer nodded. "I can't tell you what it is, but it will become evident. Soon." He smiled. "Now then, what I can tell you is…"

Marrer stalked the halls, as she did when agitated. Her power was dimming, and she raged. "The gods have interfered for the last time!"

She'd thought Berith an easy mark. Him having just lost Balala had worked in her favour, and his longing for Danu? She laughed. "Who-ever heard of a demon and a god becoming lovers?" He'd been weak and malleable.

Marrer ran her hands down Berith's chest, and he sighed. "See? You like that, don't you?"

Berith muttered, and she pushed the spell deeper, each touch and every kiss that she pushed onto his skin, marking him and erasing the memories that would get in the way of her plan.

"We're bonded, you and I. You remember that, don't you, Berith?" Her voice was guttural. "So much pleasure. It warmed you deep. So deep," she crooned, and his eyelids lowered.

"Let me lie with you again," he whispered.

Success! He'd taken the seed; he'd believe what she said and never ask a ques-tion. Zazrael would be impressed. She'd told him Berith was weak since the death of Balala.

"Remember last night, Berith. Remember the pleasure when you took me to mate. Remember the way it felt when you sank within me."

The privacy of the act had been a great assistance, and to be honest, the sex had been, if not spectacular, then enjoyable. But it had palled as the spell had slipped. Enough that he'd become aware of her other desires. *Power. "It will not slip through my fingers."*

She needed whatever that page contained, the one he sought. Surely it was either an incantation of power or some kind of spell she could utilise for her own ends?

When her demon returned to the room, she barked, "Summon my generals. We storm the library tonight." And she stalked once more to the basin, where the magic-infused blood bubbled, and slipped her fingers inside, pulling out a strand of flesh.

Danu waited in the bedroom, listening for the sounds of Berith stomping around. He'd been furious, she knew, about her actions, but she had to make him understand. Then, of course, Lucifer had arrived, and that had made things worse, not better.

"I know he felt like I betrayed him, but there were reasons," she muttered as she changed into the nightwear that was warm.

After what he'd learned she was sure he wouldn't wish to stay with her, so she'd planned for Vinta and himself to be accommodated at her temple. His other minions would be housed in locations of other gods and goddesses with whom she had friendly agreements. It was all she could manage on a short timeframe. But now, the noises from the kitchen beyond had abated, and she guessed he'd left.

Danu knew she was taking the easy way out, and that wasn't something she was overly proud of. But she didn't know if she could face his anger. Not after so many years of the coldness and distance. Better to let it melt away now, rather than continue to face the fear.

Needing to bank the fire for the night, she crept out through the door, not wanting to wake Naamah, and came face-to-face with Berith. Once more he'd assumed his human form, and she wondered, not for the first time, if he was as comfortable in that persona as his true one.

"I wondered if you'd come out at some stage," he said.

Tears pricked her eyes, and she blinked them away. "I thought you'd left."

"We need to talk, Danu."

She gulped at that. "Tea?" she muttered.

"No. Sit down, please."

It was difficult to ignore the shaking of her limbs, but she tottered to the table and sank into one of the seats. "What?"

"I've been incredibly foolish, Danu. I never saw the truth, because I wanted to believe the lie." Her eyes narrowed at his comment. "I wanted, initially at least, to relive the heady moments of my time with Balala, and it blinded me to what was there."

"I don't want your sympathy or your pity," she said. Yes, her voice was sulky, but she couldn't contain how she was feeling.

"No, I understand that…" He held up his hand. "Or I think I do." He sighed. "I let you down. I let me down too. I settled for gloss, but I should have been looking for substance. I ignored your needs, because I was, at least at the beginning, full of grief and need. Then I allowed myself to be swallowed up by the situation. I didn't ask questions."

Her laugh was bitter. "It wasn't like I really gave you a choice. I couldn't cope, so I put on the cold face, and I didn't let you close." She wasn't going to sugar-coat the truth. Besides, in her own way, she too had fed the issues between them. "I couldn't bear being near you, because I was hurting."

He winced and nodded. "Yeah, and that allowed Marrer to get a foothold because I was… I wasn't focussed on what was happening. I was too busy feeling aggrieved and sad and confused."

"Both of us were at fault," she pointed out.

"This isn't helping me come to terms with the situation," he muttered, face screwed up with self-recrimination. She reached out and touched his hand lightly, before pulling it back.

"Perhaps not, but we need to get our head in the game if we're going to beat her." Danu shook her head and conjured a cup of tea, not ready to do anything that would jeopardise the strides they'd made. The honesty was painful and yet freeing.

"So, what do we do next?" Berith asked.

"We need to find out where Fenella and Padraic and the others are up to with the planning. We need to focus on the missing page and learning what's on it."

"And what Lucifer shared?" Berith's question hung in the air between them.

She bit her lip. "I don't know that I like that all outcomes are predetermined. That argument means there's no such thing as free will." That bothered her, a lot. Did that mean that what she thought she did for good was decided by others? Or was she, as a goddess, exempted, unlike Berith? Were his feelings pre-planned by those she couldn't see?

It did gel with what she knew of the universe.

"You're discomforted by his revelations?"

"Aren't you? I mean, what if everything you said and did is decided by some unseen force? What if the emotions you feel are nothing more than a manufactured ploy to ensure an outcome neither of us can see? Doesn't that bother you?"

He stared at her. "I believe we all have free will. To some extent, things are preordained, such as the sunrise and summer. Rain and sunshine."

She sipped her tea and grimaced, it had chilled while they'd spoken. It felt like the conversation was going around in circles, and she needed time to process it. Instead, she shook her head, determined to sort out the current situation. "What are you…?"

He smiled, though his eyes were shadowed. "Tonight? I don't know, Danu. That depends on you."

She bit her lip, while her gut clenched. What did he need to know?

"I want to stay. With you. These last few days have clarified a lot of things, made me reconsider what I thought I knew. But what I want, depends on your decision, Danu."

The dam of hope in her chest was rising. Could she trust him again? Was she brave enough. "Tell me what you want, Berith. Clearly." She needed him to be totally open and honest if she was going to trust him.

"I want to stay with you. To hold you. I'm not asking for anything you're unwilling to give."

Her fingers twitched to reach out and touch him.

"I…" She licked her dry lips. "I want you to stay."

His smile was wide and warming. She rose without a word, and he followed suit. When Danu reached out, he took her hand, not tugging her close, but letting her lead the way toward the bedroom. Her fingers flicked over her shoulder, banking the fire for the night as they entered her room and closed the door.

14

Berith held Danu in the glow of morning, thankful she'd allowed him to stay. They hadn't loved, but then, he wasn't sure either of them was ready for that kind of intimacy. Not yet. Next time, he told himself, would be purposeful. He would show her the emotions coiling around his heart.

How had he ever thought himself in love with Marrer? He thought back to all the times she'd told him about how deep their connection was. Examining the events that had brought them together, for the first time, he could see the trap she'd laid.

"Berith? You didn't wait for me." The female lounged against the wall of his home. Her chest moving up and down rhythmically. Her burnished skin shining in the light. Her lips, full and red, pouted. "You promised."

"I…" He scrunched his nose. "I don't know you," he growled.

"Of course you do," and she tittered.

"No, I don't know you," he repeated.

She pushed away from the wall and advanced. "I'm Marrer, remember?"

She blinked, then wiggled her fingers. Tingles of magic slithered over his skin and invaded his brain. Memories — or were they? — uncovered, and he gasped.

"Now, you remember, yes?" she said.

He had visions of his fingers sliding over skin, kisses and heat. Emotions filling him. He blinked, because for a moment he was sure the skin was pale, the lips pink… Then that thought fled.

"My brother, Zazrael? He introduced us. Do you remember that?" She leaned in, her breasts shoving against his chest.

"Zazrael… I tutored him." He had vague recollections, seeing a young demon within the library. Introducing a female. Marrer. "I… He brought you in."

"Yes," she crooned. "He brought us together. You were so sad and lost. Then I came and you smiled. It was fated, I'm sure of it."

"Yes," he answered, "fated."

"That's right. Now here, take my token of affection." She reached out and slid an amulet around his neck. "This will remind you of how much we mean to each other," she whispered, then closed in, her lips sealing over his.

Danu stirred, opening her eyes. "Berith? You stayed."

"Yes," he said simply.

"What's wrong?" she asked with a whisper.

"Memories. I'm trying to work out how and when…"

"Marrer." Danu's face screwed up.

The name reminded him of the memory, and his hand rose, the amulet she'd given him so long ago missing. "It's gone."

"Berith?"

"Did I take it off or did I lose it?" He couldn't quite remember, only knew that now it was gone. The coldness that it seemed to feed into his body had left.

"What?" Her hand covered his. "Tell me?"

He shook his head. "No, not now. Not here." He wouldn't invade a space that was theirs with such poisonous thoughts. There was already too much to overcome. "We should rise. I've questions to ask and things to find out…"

His body arched suddenly as pain sliced through him.

"No!" His bellow was cut short as darkness filled his vision.

Danu screamed and clutched Berith to her. "Berith! Wake up," she called as his body seized in the bed beside her.

Naamah crashed into the room. "Lady Danu?"

"I need... help," she gasped. "Berith... Something's happening." Tears rolled down her cheeks, her skin suddenly frozen, as if doused with ice.

"I'll call for Vinta," Naamah said then disappeared from view.

For the first time, horror and terror filled Danu. No, they'd not yet clarified whatever was between them, but she'd had hope. To lose him now...

"Please come back to me," she crooned, smoothing her hand over his cheek. "Wake up, my love."

The door crashed open, and Lucifer strode into the room. "I told you some things were predestined. I didn't expect this quite so quickly, but..." He shrugged and advanced on the bed. "Let him go, Danu."

She stared and opened her mouth. "But..."

"Trust me, Danu. Let him go and step away."

She laid him down and backed away, hoping that this would pass quickly, whatever Lucifer was planning to do. Her fingers were twined tightly, the pain and pressure keeping a lid on the terror so it didn't spill out.

Lucifer stepped to the bed and leaned over, then he muttered something unintelligible and touched Berith on the forehead. A hum filled the air, and suddenly, Berith's eyes snapped open. His mouth opened and closed, a bit like a fish out of water. If it hadn't been so serious, she may well have laughed, but the fear filling her chest abated a little more.

"Take it easy, Berith. You'll need to lie still for a few minutes. The weight on your chest will pass in a moment or two." Then Lucifer turned to Danu. "It's done. You know about the magic of the place?"

She nodded. "Is that what...?"

"Yes and no. What I did is remove his responsibility for the library. No longer is he bound to it, and my service there. Now that it's been breached by Marrer and her minions, and you've removed your power from the shields, they failed. It was a magical snap back which caused his reaction. He needs to rest, but when Naamah returns with Vinta, have him call for me. We can talk properly then."

She nodded and noted that Lucifer hovered for a moment or two, watching Berith, then he smiled, gave a tiny nod, and stepped into the shadows.

The pallor of Berith's skin was giving way to a healthier pink tone. She breathed a little easier as he moved, eyes searching for and finding hers, and she moved closer once more.

Reaching out, their fingers entwined, she moved back close to him. "You terrified me. Don't do that again," she husked.

"Wasn't fun," he muttered, his arm moving slowly to cover his eyes. "Light hurts."

She scurried to the window and pulled close the curtains before hurrying back to him. "Better?"

"Yeah," he answered.

She glanced at Lucifer who watched with a tiny smile. "Lucifer?"

"I'll leave both of you now. Danu, when you're ready, call me and I'll give you what you're missing," he said, but she wasn't really listening as her focus was on Berith.

"Sure," she responded, still watching for any signs that Berith was going to react badly again.

Silence filled the air as Berith settled, and when his eyes closed again, it was the rise and fall of his chest that gave her a sense of peace. She stood and paced the room, her mind a whirl of concern. His reaction, if what Lucifer had said, was to the breaching of the library. Then she stilled and her mind helpfully supplied his final comments. "The bastard! He knows more than he's telling us."

Before she could say anything else, Naamah ushered Vinta into the room.

"Master?" Vinta scurried forward, and though Danu's first instinct was to stop the demon in his tracks, she didn't. He cared for Berith, so instead, she waited, allowing him to see that the demon in her bed was simply asleep now.

"He's fine, Vinta. Lucifer assured me he'd recover very soon." She kept her voice low and soothing, but slid her hands out of sight, because for all of Lucifer's words, she was still shaken to the core. She'd never really seen Berith physically affected; he was big and strong… Yes, he'd suffered with the death of Balala, but this? This was new and horrifying.

"Vinta no leave," the demon declared, and she sighed. She really didn't want him here. It was one thing to suffer his presence because of Berith's incapacitation, but another to have him in her home, which felt smaller than ever before.

"You can't stay here," she said, hoping Vinta would understand, but he got a mulish look on his face, eyes narrowed and lips tight.

"Vinta stay. Protect master."

It really was too much at this point in time, so she shrugged and glanced in the direction of Naamah. "I think a cup of tea would do all of us a world of goo—" A summons echoed, loud bongs seeming to shake the foundations of her home. "Oh no!"

"Danu?" Naamah's mouth dropped open.

Frustration and impatience warred inside her. "I can't ignore this, Naamah. Stay here. Keep an eye on Berith, and don't let him follow me." Before Naamah could respond, Danu stepped into the Dagda's presence.

"Danu, good. You're here. We've learned some very concerning news…"

15

Berith opened and closed his eyes several times in rapid succession. "What? What happened?"

Vinta came into view, and Berith blinked.

"What are you doing here?" Berith asked.

"Naamah. Master now wake."

Considering his words, even as he realised where he was, Berith struggled up onto his elbows and pierced Naamah with a glare. "Where is she?"

The demon didn't pretend not to know, and while his head ached, he was pleased she stepped closer. "Danu was summoned by the Dagda, I think. She was surprised and concerned but was clear that you're not to move from here."

He gave a grunt and made to rise, but immediately felt the weakness of his limbs and slumped back against the bed. "Is she safe?" he asked, tone anxious, because he remembered the many times she'd gone into battle, the chances she'd take to protect those that meant a lot or were weaker than herself. *And right now, that's the reality of my situation.*

Naamah cocked her head. "I believe so. Something is happening, and she's not happy." She shrugged. "It's hard to read her emotions, I have so little experience, and the distance... It's an odd side effect to this bond we have."

Berith closed his eyes, wishing he could be by Danu's side while she faced whatever there was to come.

Danu settled into the seat at the Dagda's urging.

"I have news. It's not good, but neither is it insurmountable."

"Okay," she muttered. "What do you know?" She wiggled in the chair, pushing her backside into a comfortable position.

"We understand the library has been breached." The Dagda settled himself opposite her and waited.

"I... Yes, that's the case."

"And that Berith has absented himself from those premises?"

She certainly couldn't argue that but was discomforted as there was clearly something he wanted to know. "I... That's also true."

"There are no further shields around the library?"

She squinted at the man before her. "You're hedging, brother. What do you really want to know?"

"It's not what I want to know, per se. There's a book. A tome." His fingers gripped the chair's arms, knuckles turning white.

"And?" She was starting to feel the rising of concern in her gut. "What about it?"

Dagda sighed. "When we first came, we were required to submit certain knowledge in order to remain. The truth about why we were made to leave our home."

Now Danu sucked in a deep breath. "Do you mean to say...?"

"Aye. The knowledge of our eviction from the other place is in that book. The knowledge of what our master would become too. It must be protected." He pushed forward, nearly invading her chair space. "That tome, it's blue and green. The pages are painted with silver. It was meant to be kept hidden."

Lucifer's words haunted her. *'When you're ready, call me and I'll give you what you're missing,'* replayed in her mind. She tapped her fingers to her forehead. "He played me. He played us both," she muttered.

"You must retrieve it, Danu. Reclaim your mantle of warrior and enter the library. Send it back so we may protect the knowledge."

She nodded. "I will, but I need to do something first." She rose and made to leave the room, but stopped and glanced over her shoulder. "I'll be back, but when this is done, things need to change."

Then she was in her home, stalking toward the bedroom.

"Vinta!" she yelled.

His head popped through her doorway.

"I need to know the location of a blue and green book. The pages are edged in silver."

His eyes widened. "Closed," he muttered. "Need key."

She held out her hand, and he shook his head. "Give me the key, Vinta. I must retrieve it."

"In library. Marrer…" His eyes darted from side to side, and his forked tongue licked at his lips.

"Give me the key. I'll make sure it's secured before I leave, but that book… It's dangerous," she muttered.

Berith lumbered into the kitchen. "Where've you been? And you can't go in there, it's dangerous."

With a sigh, Danu used a thought to change her attire, and Vinta stared at her. "I don't have a choice. I must retrieve that book. It contains things that… Well, if Marrer gets it, then not just this world is in trouble," she muttered, patting her sword at her side.

"Danu," warned Berith.

"I'm a warrior," she reminded him. "It's my role and task to protect, just as much as my other titles." And while many considered her soft and caring, a goddess of childbirth, it was her other, more hidden side that she embraced now. The one dressed in black with silver-tipped gloves and a sword that she'd wielded for centuries. The mask she'd fit before battle hung from leather straps from her scabbard.

"I'll come with you," Berith growled.

"No. But when I come back, Lucifer, you, and I will be talking about what the hell he knows." She plucked the key from Vinta's outstretched hand, glad she didn't have to forcefully retrieve it.

"Danu…" Naamah called as she entered the room, then stilled.

"I'll return," she said and took advantage of the confusion of the room to leave.

Marrer stalked the length of the library. "Find me the book! There must be something in there to tell me what is on the page!"

She hadn't been inside these walls for a long time, but not much had really changed. Berith's office, a large room to the rear, was still as dull and ugly as it was before. The oak desk stank of must, and the leather chair didn't appear to have changed either.

A decanter caught the light, and she snarled, snatching it up and removing the stopper. She guzzled the spirits within before throwing it at the wall. It smashed and the pieces dropped down with a satisfying tinkle.

"I will destroy you," she muttered. "All those years I waited for you to give me what I desired, all those times you denied me access and power. You'll pay."

Her eyes scanned the room, and she advanced, her fingers reaching for and gripping the image in a frame. It was a painting of Danu. Rough and crude but clear. She hurled it at the wall and laughed.

"I'll smash you too, Danu. Your power will be puny once I gain what is rightly mine!"

She laughed, the sound discordant, and she slid to the floor. Her memories of a time lost to humans rolled back.

Marrer sat at the foot of her father, the great demon Asmodeus. He was the demon of lust, and she was yet another borne of that dark desire. "Father, tell me of the world," she entreated, and he smiled, but it wasn't indulgent as yet another woman entered the room, this time carrying another child. A dark child, male.

"A son, my lord. An heir," the woman muttered and laid the child on his lap.

"A son?" He snarled, glancing down.

When it mewled, Marrer was sure he'd demand it be taken away, but he didn't. Instead, it waved arms and legs as if reaching toward him. Then it levitated and she felt the first stirrings of something old and heavy inside her.

"A boy," her father breathed reverentially. "With immense magic already. You've done well, Velina. I shall raise him, keep him near, and he shall be my heir."

Marrer clambered from the floor at his feet, already aware that this was unusual and likely a threat. "I'm your heir," she reminded him. "You told me so."

Asmodeus glanced down at her, lips misshapen into a sneer. "You were until I had him. Now he is my heir, and you will be silent. You are a girl, a vessel only to carry those borne of magic. You have no future now, except as a consort. You will be schooled in the ways of lust, and you will be thankful I did not drown you at birth, as I have so many others." He glanced to his minion. "Watch him well, she will be a threat, and nothing… nothing, shall harm this child. He will take control of everything one day. Take her to the harem accommodations and see that her ability to control and use magic is bound. I will not have the threat here in my own home."

The minion bowed low and grabbed her arm.

Struggling, Marrer fought, but he dragged her from the throne room. Even as a youngling, Marrer was no fool. She'd lost her father's favour with her outburst. She'd make the best of her opportunities, but they wouldn't bind her. She was already considering how to stop that as she was removed from the place she wanted to be.

Even now, those memories seared her. The boy-child had taken everything from her: her father, her place, and her future. It didn't matter that their father had passed a century ago, and not even at her own hand. Her father had decreed she would never again hold the title of heir. He'd raised three other worthy and power-filled sons before his death, and she'd been pushed down the line with each birth.

But soon enough she'd have more power than her father could have ever dreamed of, and those who'd stolen her birthright would pay. Berith had been merely a pawn, and one she'd all but drained dry. And that bitch Danu? She too would have to be dealt with to ensure that no one and nothing stopped Marrer's plans.

Pushing up from the floor, she reconsidered the room and stomped out of it.

16

Danu entered the library on silent feet, glancing to the left and the right but remaining low.

The flagstones on the floor would have been noisy if she'd chosen other shoes except these well-worn boots, and she was thankful she hadn't yet done anything about replacing them.

The layout of the area was one she knew well. To the left she entered a small reading room, and to the right was an antechamber that led to a room where books, aged and well-used, were repaired.

The flickering of lights above her reminded her that Berith was a traditionalist, preferring candles to electricity. They may be in the underworld, but certain human inventions had been warmly received by facets of the demonic society. Not for the first time did the irony of this make her smile, but that was swiftly banished.

She was here to get the book and get out of there. She noted the way books and scrolls were scattered on the floor, telling her Marrer had beaten her to the library.

A scuttle had her dashing for a table and diving beneath it as a small demon scurried by, carrying more books. "Mistress says not the ones," it chattered to the second demon following behind.

"Not our problem. We find books, we deliver to Velifar, and we return."

Velifar was a strange demon for Marrer to employ, Danu thought. A demon of deception… She suddenly understood. They were looking for a book disguised as something else, perhaps even a scroll.

She waited impatiently, keeping an eye on the far end of the room, where her hourglass sat. She glanced at it and smiled. It was clear Vinta kept the library in tip-top condition because the room glowed under the dancing candlelight. But that pleasure died away, because she needed to get to that end of the room, unseen.

Moving to the edge of the table, she listened. No sound, so she scurried to dive under the next table just as the demons returned, dumping more books on a table before collecting others from the shelf.

Berith would have a fit if he saw the mess they were making. If she could, she'd clear them out, but right now wasn't the time. Her mission was clear—find that book. The key in her pocket burned, and the longer she took, the greater the danger.

Danu crept from table to table, four down and only one left when she heard the voice.

"Why haven't you found it yet?" Marrer was strident, and Danu shrank deeper within the cover, hoping to evade notice.

Just beyond was Berith's office and off that the restricted book area. It was where she needed to access, but with Marrer stalking the room, she was unable to move forward or back.

Glancing around, she knew there was no other option except to wait for Marrer to leave, so she settled herself carefully out of sight, letting her muscles relax. Long, cramped hours weren't unknown to her, but if she could be reasonably comfortable, she would be able to move swiftly when the time came. Instead of needing to unfold aching legs and arms, she'd be able to move immediately.

Marrer bellowed and cursed, calling the minions she had at her service all manner of things, yet they still didn't find what was sought. Nor did they breach the restricted section, which Berith and Vinta had told her in the past was hidden and well-protected, and Danu breathed a sigh of relief.

Time passed, and Danu waited. Finally, Marrer declared, "I must feed," and left.

The atmosphere in the library lightened a little, as if whatever wove itself around Marrer infected the air, and Danu inhaled deeply, knowing time was limited.

Assured she was alone in the room, she made a dash to the entrance of Berith's office, but pulled up, noting the mess. "Oh no," she whispered, then closed her mouth and glanced over her shoulder. *At least no one heard me.*

As much as she wanted to clear the mess, time was of the essence, so she made her way to the far end of the room, felt the tingle of Berith's energy, and slid her fingers over the walls of hewn rock. *What you cannot see, you can feel,* he'd told her long years ago, and she relied now on that sense to find the lock and slide the key inside.

The magic dropped as the door opened, and she stepped into the tiny room.

Rows of shelves were filled with titles, and she looked this way and that, until on the lowest shelf to the left, in the middle, she spied what she hunted for. Her fingers shook as she traced the title, *True Tailes of Tuatha De Danaan Travels.*

There was little time to waste, but she hurried back to Berith's office, and once more closed and locked the restricted section. She was aware of the restrictions he'd placed on the room—not quite wards, but a magic restraint—and she would need to plan her next move carefully. At any time, someone might well come looking and she was best to use magic to send the book back to the one who could control the information within.

Berith's magical hold and wards were looser than usual on the room, but strong enough she couldn't transport herself directly from here. The sense of urgency had her using more magic than she would ordinarily, but at least the book was away, sent to the Dagda. She exhaled and an external sound intruded.

She spun and sighed. "Damn," she muttered.

In the doorway, grinning at her, was Velifar. "Well, hello, Danu. Long time, no visit," the demon drawled, while her eyes glowed and her teeth shone in the dim light. Danu didn't look at the long length of nails she also was sure had extruded from meaty fingertips.

Danu's hand slipped over the hilt of her sword. "There's a dampener in this room," she muttered.

Velifar cocked her head. "Yes, but it didn't stop you poofing away whatever that was."

Danu growled, her hand wrapping around the grip and sliding it up with a savage hiss as sword left scabbard. "You're mighty chatty today, Velifar. You know, I never took you as someone who would natter to their death."

Velifar growled and shot toward her, face twisted with fury. "You bitch! It's not my death we'll celebrate today."

Danu sidestepped. "My, if that's your best..." she goaded.

A hand, tipped with long, black claws, swung at her. "I'm going to rip you to pieces, then Marrer will devour your flesh, and I'll be her second!" Wind rippled where the swipe just missed Danu's ear.

"I don't think so," muttered Danu as she danced in a circle, evading once more the advance of the demon.

She knew Velifar of old. The creature was quick and weighty, but she would soon begin to slow. Danu remembered what she'd read, that the demon exhibited initial speed, but once the first burst of adrenaline was expended, she would puff and pant. Danu knew that only then would she become easy to distract and to defeat. She hoped what she read was correct anyway. All Danu needed to do in the first instance was evade for as long as possible and remain out of reach.

But in the smaller space of the office, that was difficult, as she slid and slipped on the floor, attempting to dodge both Velifar and the detritus.

A claw connected and pain ricocheted through Danu's arm.

"First blood," crowed the demon.

"And the last I'll shed for you," she replied, now swinging her sword in a speedy but graceful arc. It struck hard and deep, and Velifar snarled.

The deadly waltz continued, with swinging and dodging, sliding and twisting. She shut out the sounds of Velifar's threats and goads, realising there was nothing in it she wanted or needed to hear. The demon's reliance on fear was a tactic Danu had seen many times before in the past. *I need to use it against her.*

More than once the demon sliced at Danu, connecting and drawing blood, which now began to run freely, making her movements more difficult and deadly. However, she too laid blows on her foe, and Velifar was bleeding freely.

But as Velifar lumbered once more toward her, Danu's back was against the desk. She knew the time had come for the fatal blow, as the demon lurched up toward her, Velifar's mouth hanging open, Danu sucked in oxygen.

Now or never, Danu told herself, and instead of the arc Velifar expected, she shunted the blade out and into Velifar's chest. It sank deep with a sucking sound. Her face turned slack, and the claws grabbed for Danu's arms. Held her, nails diving deep into flesh and sinews.

Crying out in pain wasn't an option, she wouldn't give the demon that reward, so she shook and pasted a snarling smile on her face. "Got you," Danu muttered.

Her body ached, but the sounds of the battle had drawn more foes, and she rounded on the doorway, where three more lesser demons waited, slavering.

"Ugh," Danu muttered, but she knew going through them without engaging wouldn't gain her freedom.

She advanced with slow and sure steps and prepared to meet those waiting by the door. Her smile must have told them that she'd make them pay, because the smallest gave a squeak and decamped. The largest growled, and Danu rolled her eyes. "Like I haven't seen your kind and destroyed them before."

Her snarl had no real effect as the creature extended claws and razor-sharp teeth.

She swung a gentle arc, though her grip wasn't quite what she needed to destroy or overcome it. Her brain helpfully suggested that all she needed to do was get out of the office.

The demon facing her obviously didn't know her plans, and she was grateful that even in her pain-filled haze they couldn't read her intentions, particularly given she was slower and less graceful in her movements. They were moving backward and forward, engaging with the sword, while her moves were designed to get her through the doorway and beyond the wards.

I'm going to be in trouble if I don't get out of here soon. A black cloud was starting to obscure her vision, and she had no intention of allowing any of Marrer's minions to take her captive.

She moved forward, and the buzz of the wards told her she was out. She raised a hand. "Later," she growled and stepped through the fold in space.

Berith grunted, wondering where the hell Danu was. Yes, she'd been dressed for battle, and in his weakened state, he would have been no help, but it didn't settle his concerns.

When she reappeared, he cursed and caught her as she fell. "Danu!"

Her lids fluttered. "Hi," she whispered. "I'm a bit bloody."

"You're a bloody idiot," he muttered, holding her close. Heaven knew she appeared battered, and whatever she'd done, it had been accomplished without his assistance. It made him feel surplus to requirements, and he didn't like that one bit!

"Nice, Berith. But I'm bleeding all over the floor."

He pulled away and noted the tears in her clothing, the way she wobbled on her feet, and the chalkiness of her skin.

"Velifar was a bit more capable than I expected," she muttered, and his frown deepened.

"Velifar? Marrer's executioner?"

She nodded and plucked at her clothing. "Can we continue this after I bathe and we sort out my healing?"

He grunted and turned her toward the bedroom. "Naamah? Fix tea and something filling, we might be a while." He slid the door shut behind them and unbuckled Danu's belt, relieving her of sword and scabbard. A thought occurred, stopping him in his tracks. He turned her toward him, urgency infusing his words, "Did she bite you?"

"Uh, no. But at the end, she sank her claws in."

He tore at her clothes until she stood before him nude. He inspected her body, sliding fingers over the blemishes on her skin and cursing at the streaks of dark green and black marring the fine texture of flesh. "We need to clarify your tissues," he said and leaned down, sliding his mouth over the wounds.

"What are you…?" she said, shock filling her exclamation.

"Wait," he muttered, then sucked, feeling the frigid slide of the poison he was removing from her. As he checked between draws, he noted the way the streaks receded and kept at it, working wound by wound. Then swallowing and sliding his tongue over the entry points. "My saliva will defuse the effects of the poison," he explained.

"That's kind of gross… in a hot way," she murmured, and he glanced up, noting her soft and lush curves, her nipples tight little buds.

He squeezed his eyes shut, because his body wanted something neither of them were in the kind of position to act on. "Let's get you bathed," he muttered.

"But Berith," she crooned. "Please?"

He sighed. "You're not in your normal mind, Danu. My saliva mixed with the venom is like a chemical mix, and it's affecting your rational thought."

He waved his hand over the tub so it filled with warm water, and he carefully slid her into it.

"Oh," she sighed and shivered.

"Too cold?" His voice had a distinctly gravelled quality.

"Sooo nice," she moaned, and her eyes closed as she clenched her legs together.

His face flamed. She didn't thrash or moan, but the way her face tightened and the muscles of her long neck pulled taut told him she was lost in the throes of orgasm.

He panted, because the utter pleasure rolled off her in carnal waves and his human-shaped body ached to join her in fulfilment.

He held firm and waited until she slumped, then her eyes opened, still glassy but there was awareness in their depths. "Oh dear," she whispered, cheeks flaming. "I need to get out of here." She pushed up, and his eyes followed her form, the way the water sluiced down her body.

"Yeah," he growled and grabbed a towel from the ornately curved rack. He thrust it at her then turned away, because he refused to embarrass himself with the way his cock jutted against his pants.

He heard her drying then dressing. "Uh, Berith?"

He glanced over his shoulder and noted the pink of her cheeks.

"I'm... Uh, I didn't mean to embarrass you," she said.

"You didn't," he muttered.

"Then what?"

He turned, took her hand, and placed it against his erection.

"Oh," she said. "Well, then." She gave a nod. "I guess..."

He cocked his head to the side. "We should go eat, and you need a hot drink." He steered her toward the kitchen and waited for her to sit before he followed suit.

Naamah seemed to taste the tension in the air, and she remained silent and settled about making some food and drinks.

17

Danu ate in relative silence, feeling as if she'd somehow crossed a boundary she shouldn't have.

Her mind spun in circles, because she'd learned such a lot in the last few days, not just about herself and Berith, but also the wider situation, and she really needed to understand it all. She also needed to make some decisions.

She'd kept Padraic on a string for centuries, but the reality was, that wasn't something she'd enjoyed. It had been a necessary evil centuries ago, giving him the support of being one of her generals, but also ensuring her need to remain relevant was fulfilled. He'd never seen it like that, only believing she was keeping him for her own needs.

It had been her choice, true, that Padraic think she was a selfish being. Of course, selfishness came with her position, but she was neither as unaware nor uncaring as she allowed him to think. But times and needs had changed.

I don't really need to keep up the façade anymore.

She also needed to consider her future—if she had one, that was. The situation with Berith had muddied those waters. And where did the situation with them lead? She cast a covert glance in his direction.

He'd claimed to love her. Knowing now that Marrer had somehow made him forget their bond had left her broken. What if something similar happened again?

Her options were bipolar. She could take the chance, or she could fade. There didn't appear to be any in-between for her.

Berith reached across the table and took her hand. "You're thinking."

Her head snapped up. "Yes. I need to make some decisions, Berith."

"Not including fading?"

She stared at him, because how could she possibly answer that? Fading was still in her mind, but telling him that was… She didn't want him to feel guilty, nor to feel a sense of responsibility. This decision was hers, and hers alone.

"I have a lot to think over," she answered finally, and didn't miss his frown. "It's my choice, Berith. Now, I'm tired, so perhaps I'll retire." She pushed the chair back and rose.

He followed her.

"What are you doing?" she asked.

"If you're retiring, then so am I," he answered.

Confusion raced through her. "Why?" The word slipped out before she could stop it. She stepped toward the door.

He shook his head, his face screwed up into a half-grimace, half-smile. "Because where you are is where I need to be. It's where I belong."

The words stopped her in her tracks. She turned, her eyes searching his. Looking for what she was unsure of. She was somewhat aware that Naamah scurried from the room, but it wasn't of importance, because everything she needed was potentially before her.

"Tell me what you're saying. Make it clear, Berith."

His hands reached for and gripped her shoulders. "I want you, Danu. I want everything forever. I don't ever want to leave you again."

Danu wanted to believe what he was saying, but she was terrified to trust him fully again.

"Danu?"

"I do want to believe you, honestly. But I... You hurt me before, and I don't know..." She looked down, lacing her fingers together.

"I need to earn your trust. I understand that." He spoke with a quiet earnestness that she could believe, which was paired with a slow nod.

"I need time, Berith. If you want to prove your commitment to me, it will take time. But while time passes, we have other, more difficult, things to consider."

He raised a brow.

"How to defeat Marrer."

He grunted. "She's like a bad smell."

Danu smiled. "That she is, but she's one we have to eliminate."

Berith held Danu as she slept, pleased that her wounds were healing quickly now that the venom had been removed.

Thoughts crowded his mind, including how they were going to defeat Marrer. It was true, with the loss of Velifar, their side had a greater chance than before, and the loss of both Zazrael and Ate as her walking, talking, magic battery were severe blows to her army. But was it enough?

In the morning he'd have to check in on Padraic's crew. Maybe they'd have news for him. Something needed to give soon, because he knew the strain was telling on Danu. Oh, she'd refute that, no doubt, but she was wearing thin. Between that, the mess he'd made of things, and her upcoming decision, so much hung in the balance.

He squeezed his eyes shut. He hated this loss of power. He detested relying on others. And watching Danu leave him safe in her little home while she retrieved the book? That had infuriated him.

Even worse was the knowledge that the battles she faced weren't of her own choosing, nor were the secrets being kept from both of them.

Lucifer's words were dim too, after the attack on the library had severed his connection with that venerable space. He couldn't be totally sure of what he'd said, but he had a vague recollection of some-thing more that wasn't being shared. It all added up to dark shades of nothing and more.

Danu stirred. "Berith?"

"Yes, my love," he muttered. "Go back to sleep."

She snorted softly. "You're thinking too loud."

He laughed at her words. "Then what should I do?" He waited as she stilled, her eyes shining in the dim light, the fire flickering in the hearth.

"Love me," she whispered.

"I do, and I will. Forever." He turned and leaned over her, his lips touching hers.

When Berith kissed Danu, it was soft and sweet. Inside her chest, something unfurled, like the petals on a rose. Soft and fragile, yet beautiful. She raised her hand, cupping his cheek, feeling the warmth of his skin.

"Show me the real you," she whispered.

He stilled. "It's ugly," he muttered.

"No, it's not," she told him. "It's you. Both parts of you, Berith." Maybe this was why they'd never breached the divide between them? He'd been too afraid to show her both sides of himself, and she'd never understood that it was her role to show him they both were equally important. "I love every part of you, every face you show."

"How can you love this face?" And he let it morph to the black-skinned, red-eyed creature of nightmares.

"I never feared that side of you Berith," she whispered, sliding a finger over his black, leathery lips. "Because I never feared you. I mourned your absence from my life, but first, you were my friend, then my lover. I don't look at what you present on the outside, but rather the being that is inside. Your heart and soul."

He closed his eyes. "I still don't remember that time," he muttered.

She rested her forehead against his and whispered, "I know. But even if you never remember, I will. But instead, we'll make new memories," she said, and her eyes widened.

"Danu?"

"Love me," she muttered, arching against his body, and he let go of the magic allowing him to be human and demon. This time it was his body, hard and hot, that pushed against her. His claws that gently held her form against his.

He kissed her, taking care not to nip too hard as his serrated teeth slid over her soft, warm flesh.

"I feel you," she whispered. "Your heat and strength, and your need."

He had to close his eyes as her voice called like a siren to the deepest and most hidden part of himself. If anyone had told him previously that demons had souls, he would have scoffed at them, but now? He felt their connection as his lips ravaged hers.

"I want to be one with you," he panted against her neck.

"No one wants that more than me," she whispered, nearly overcome with the emotions swelling inside her. Love, hunger, lust, and hope warred for the upper hand. She slid her hand through the air and the ripple of magic stole the clothing that kept their bodies separated. "Love me, now," she demanded.

His fingers slid down her body. "But you need—"

"You," she finished, sliding one leg over his muscular hip, toes touching the length of his tail, sliding down it, so that he arched. She knew the places that would goad him into action, and she used that knowledge, pushing him to fill her, because her body needed the connection as much as her heart did.

Finally, he pushed inside her body, filling her, and she gasped at the pleasure that radiated through her.

"Berith…" The word escaped her lips as her eyes fluttered closed.

"Need," he muttered, "need you." And he kissed her, deeply, his tongue sliding against hers and fluttering so that true thought fled.

Inside her body, the coil of heat raged to a furnace, and she moved and undulated, his nails sliding into her flesh as he met her thrust for thrust.

Her mind splintered, the orgasm roaring through her, a torrent of pleasure, and he cried out too. "I love you," he growled.

Tears slid down her cheeks. She wanted to accept the words, but was she brave enough?

"I love you, Berith. I always have and always will." She made the words a vow and hoped he'd understand the importance as he gathered her close. "Don't leave me, never again," she muttered.

"I won't," he murmured, settling her body, still dewy with perspiration and heart running a million miles an hour, against him.

She inhaled the scent of him, allowing it to centre her.

"I will be here, by your side, for eternity." His fingers slid through her hair, and she closed her eyes. "Sleep now," he whispered, and she let go of reality.

A ripple echoed through the cavern, and Marrer snarled. "Why? He was mine!"

Her screech set the minions in the room shaking.

She felt the instant Berith broke the last thread of magic holding him to her. "That bitch!" she screamed, spittle flying. "He was supposed to be mine for eternity, my minion, my prisoner. Bound only to me!"

The moment she'd first laid eyes on Danu, she'd known that it was her role to steal what belonged to the tall goddess. Danu had been gifted with deep magic, vibrant red hair and ruby lips, and a body that screamed of perfection, and she'd had everything, while Marrer? She'd been nothing. A scrap of a demon with little magic and no future to hope for.

Danu's hair shone in the sunlight, and while they'd been in the shade, it was a beacon demanding Marrer's attention. Beside her, on the log, was a male demon. As she watched, he plucked a flower from the garden and handed it to Danu who smiled.

"Get along with you, minion," roared one of the overseers who served the great demon king, Astaroth.

The chains on her wrists and ankles bit deep as the others made to move, yet she remained still, transfixed by the sight before her. Moving from one part of the demon kingdom to the other sometimes required them to traverse the upperworld. Today was one of those rare opportunities.

"Who is that?" she asked as she trudged forward, her service to the partner of the king about to begin after she'd been surrendered in lieu of service to the king of battles and the eater of souls.

"That? That's Berith, the master of the library of the underworld and second to Lucifer himself. Now get on." And the slash of the whip had torn the skin of her hide, and she snarled. "Get on!" the overseer bellowed as she started forward again.

Whatever the woman had, she'd one day demand. If only she could find her way out of servitude, Marrer told herself as they stepped once more in to the darkness beyond.

In that moment, everything the goddess had was an afront to Marrer. A reminder that she'd forever be little more than a plaything, unless she planned, so she had, beguiling the youngest son of her mistress.

Sitri been so besotted that she'd be freed and there'd been some talk that perhaps he'd make her his mate. Not that he'd been what she desired. The day she'd captured Berith's attention slid before her half-closed eyes.

Sitri scurried forward. "We've been summoned," he panted.

"Summoned, where?" she asked. Until she'd either mated him or moved on, she couldn't afford to tip her hand or show her dissatisfaction.

"Astaroth has been summoned to the great library. We're to accompany him."

She licked her lips but held back the smile that wanted to escape. Finally!

She smoothed the gown she wore, adjusted it, while ensuring the amulet she'd acquired was hidden between her breasts. Unlike many demons, she had an almost human form, and she knew many demons found that desirable. Never had she thanked her stars that an ancestor had taken a human lover, at least until now. She'd learned, long ago, that only the strongest could take a human form, unless there was a latent thread of human in their lineage.

"Come," Sitri urged, and she allowed him to lead her from the cavern. If he thought he was somehow in charge of them, she'd let him go. Soon, she'd have bigger prey to hunt.

Entering the library was a revelation. She welcomed the smell of must and decay as she was led toward her target. Berith was settled with a lesser demon beside him. She'd learned of Vinta, but all her attempts to interact had been rebuffed.

Sitri made the introduction, and she smiled in what she hoped was a seductive manner.

Berith acknowledged her, though his attention was clearly split, and she remembered that day, almost a century earlier, when she'd spied Berith and the human-looking goddess. The one with the perfect hair and body and the red lips and who'd taken the flower from his hand.

"My lord, Berith." She dropped down low into a curtsey, which allowed him a glimpse of her cleavage, barely contained within the straps of her dress.

"Uh, Sitri and Marrer," he muttered, only acknowledging them in minimally proper form.

"Yes," she said and blinked as he turned away. Fury scored her, because she'd plotted so long to reach this point.

Mine. The thought echoed through her, and she surreptitiously reached for the amulet while adjusting herself. As she bowed low once more, on the pretext of sidling away, Marrer slid the item onto his lap.

He'd jerked as the metal made contact, his eyes returning to her. "Marrer?" he'd queried, and she'd smiled.

In that moment, Sitri was forgotten, and her plan started to take shape.

But now, the magic loop was broken, and she felt it. The snapping of the last connection between them.

The time of battle was looming. Soon, she'd take control again, and this time, he wouldn't escape her.

18

Berith rose and dressed before light broke. He felt good. Full of vigour and hope. In the kitchen, he set the stove and the kettle to boil. He'd arrange a breakfast for Danu... Once Naamah came downstairs to show him how.

Strange, he'd never before considered Danu's life. He remembered all the times she'd showered him with kindness. A warming drink when the weather left him aching with cold, or a meal to fill his insides after poring over books or preparing a news binding.

Memories were slowly returning, and each one was examined and savoured.

Naamah entered the kitchen not long after he'd settled at the table. "My lord." She bowed to him.

"I've been relieved of my duty," he told Naamah who watched him.

"Even so, my Lady Danu has taken me to serve her. She's granted me a future. I will treat her mate with the respect that you once showed me."

He smiled. "Perhaps we consider once a year you can acknowledge me, because it's going to be awfully busy if every time I call you, you bow and scrape."

Naamah blushed. "If that is your wish, my lord?" But her grin was impish, and he laughed.

"Come, show me how to fashion a breakfast for Danu."

She sighed. "So you've known Danu for over a millennia, yet you don't know what she eats for breakfast?"

He growled, "Clearly not. It's my opportunity to correct that."

They worked together, and when Danu entered the room, her look of surprise was a delight to him.

They sat down to a companionable meal, at least until Lucifer turned up. Naamah took the opportunity to decamp, so once more three were gathered around the table.

"You visited the library, Danu?" Lucifer's booming voice was hushed. "That's good. You found the book?"

She sighed. "Yes, I did, but I have a bone to pick with you."

He nodded. "I know. I couldn't give you all the information immediately. You should understand this, given your own, somewhat difficult, story of how you came here."

Berith watched her wince.

"Yes, I do, but you owe Berith an explanation." Danu wiggled in her chair.

"Indeed, I do. That's what I'm here to attend to now. When I left, I told you I'd explain the rest, including the truth about the missing page."

Berith leaned in. "You know where it is?"

Lucifer nodded slowly. "Yes, I do. It's here."

Danu shook her head. "You said we'd need to call you. If I remember correctly, you said 'call me and I'll give you what you're missing,' but you seem to know exactly what's going on here, in my home."

Lucifer smiled and nodded. "It's not so much that I know, it's that it's all foretold."

Berith growled his frustration with the demon lord. "It's amazing that somehow everything is foretold, yet nothing we need to know is told to us ahead of time." His long claws tapped on the scarred, wooden tabletop.

Lucifer sighed, glancing at the nails bouncing up and down. "I don't make these rules, Berith."

"So, what don't we know?" Danu asked, and Berith knew she was trying to steer the discussion back on track.

Lucifer held out a hand and in it appeared a page. The edges were torn and the page scrunched up.

"Is that...?" breathed Danu.

"It is," he muttered and handed the sheet to Danu.

She read the page, paled, and handed the paper to Berith.

Long ago, decisions were made. Choices enacted. Hearts broken. The price paid in pain.

Things that came to pass. These are foretold and cannot be changed.

There will be a time random of place but known of time, that the losses of the one known as Berith will come to pass. Each loss is known and grieved but necessary.

Each loss shall build the character of the demon known as Berith until such time as the knowledge of his evolution will be clear. It will teach him much and open his mind to what may come to pass. They will strengthen and gird him.

Lucifer shall be the one who will make the announcement. This shall be at a time when the presence of the Lady Danu clarifies the relationship between them.

Berith shall consort with the Lady Danu, and those who owe her fealty, to overcome the danger to both the upper and underworlds. Their connection must be clear before the announcement is made.

They must work together with all those they have connections to, as the danger is clear and the outcome unknown. Should they fail, all will end, and humanity will be lost.

Berith didn't quite know how to approach the words inscribed on the page, but he felt the power of them.

"What does this mean by the 'evolution'?" Berith pointed to the word on the page.

Lucifer smiled. "I know you felt the second your connection to the library was severed. That was also foretold, though in another prophecy." Lucifer shrugged. "It's difficult yet positive news, but we knew that was the moment that your evolution was concluded. No longer shall you be a demon. You may not have physically changed, but no longer are you mine to direct. You have ascended to a higher status, Berith. The gods know that you have given good and true service, and in recognition, they are asking that you take over as Cernunnos."

"Cernunnos?" Danu said. "But he's…"

Berith's mouth had dropped open at Lucifer's pronouncement, and Danu's query had him wide-eyed. "But Cernunnos isn't aged or unwell. So why…?"

Lucifer shook his head. "No, he's not, but he no longer wishes to fulfill the role. Certain roles must be filled to ensure the balance of positive and negative energies, which ensure the balance of this world. Cernunnos has filled the position for more years than he'd wish to admit to, but he's wearied of it. He, and we, all the powers that be, believe you'd be excellent at filling the vacancy. The Dagda, Cressida, and the head of the coven all believe you'd offer us honest and effi-cient service."

"But… I'm a demon."

Danu reached out and gripped his hands. "Lucifer?"

Lucifer grinned. "Yes and no. I mean, you wouldn't look any differ-ent, and since you easily take on human form as demon, it's not too great a stretch for you to look the part of Cernunnos."

Excitement rolled through his veins. "And the library?"

Lucifer sighed. "Yes, based on Danu's information, it's a big mess. It will take time to clear and rebuild what is there, but you've trained your successor well."

"Successor?" He sounded like a bloody parrot. His fingers clenched tight as he worked through the reality of how stupid he felt.

"Vinta," breathed Danu. "That's who you mean, isn't it?"

"Yes," answered Lucifer. "But as much as it's an opportunity to evolve for yourself, there's one more aspect to this. The powers and skills of Cernunnos will be useful in the battle against Marrer."

"Balala knew this?" Berith's chest ached for the woman he'd loved and lost and the child as well.

Lucifer nodded slowly. "She knew you were meant for greater things, and she mourned the loss of your shared future, but she loved you. Enough to let go of her dreams and life."

Danu's hand settled on his. Warming him, and a salve to his aching soul.

"Cernunnos himself is aware and agrees with our decision." Lucifer shook his head. "He was aware of the prophecy."

"You had the page all along, didn't you?" Danu leaned forward.

"Yes and no. Yes, I knew where it was, it's part of the reason I withdrew, because the time was essential. As you read it here, it couldn't be found too soon. But no, while Balala was the one who accessed it for me, I gave her the ability to hide it here, in Danu's home, I did not hide it myself." Lucifer clasped his hands together and glanced down. "When she came to you, Danu, it was to protect herself and the child, but also to undertake the task of secreting the page here. Not in any visible location, but in the very air. She knew you were both meant to be. That her part to play was only for a season."

Berith felt a mix of fury and sorrow gathering. "You used Balala."

"No, I didn't. She and the child couldn't and wouldn't survive. Even with the power and magic that Danu was feeding her, it was only a matter of time before she passed. The human body isn't meant to contain such things for more than a limited period, which you already know, Berith. It's like the vampires and were. Once the journey of change begins, there must be a physical alteration creating a new being, so the magic is contained and safe. But demons don't make new demons, not at the level you were. Lesser demons can impregnate humans, but even then, it takes a toll on the human carrier. But stronger demons must have a mate with an existing thread of power, either a demon hybrid or something similar."

Berith heard the words, knew what he was being told, but he still felt the innate loss.

"They will be forever in your heart, Berith," Danu whispered. "No one will ever ask you to forget them."

A breeze slid over his cheek, and for a moment, he could swear it was a shade of Balala. Tears filled his eyes. "I understand this. I just wish…"

"You have a new opportunity, Berith. As Cernunnos, you can have a family. Children."

"With Danu," Berith whispered and heard her inhale. He turned, speared her with his gaze. "I love you, Danu. I always have, but that's changed, become more. With you, I want forever."

She smiled, a tremulous movement of her lips, but in her gaze, he read her acceptance of the words.

Lucifer cleared his throat. "Yes, well… That's great and all, but you need to see Padraic, gather your troops, because my connections have informed me that Marrer is moving. She's lost Zazrael, she's lost Velifar, and she's lost Ate. She won't wait much longer, because as she weakens, her grip on power is ebbing. She'll need to move while she can still command her generals. Once they get wind that she's weakening…"

"She won't wait, you're right. I need to see Padraic, Grace, Luke, and Fenella. And if what you've said and what's on that page is right," Danu said with a sigh, "we'll need Cressida, and the vampires, and the lycans too."

Berith reached for her hand. "Together."

19

Danu ate slowly, preparing to meet her newly created council of war. Padraic had summoned Cressida, and her strongest allies, the lycans, were massing from every corner of the globe and her own, the leprechauns, fae, and fairies along with the witches of her regions were already on-site.

Gulping a last sip of her coffee, Danu willed herself dressed in the black uniform of a warrior. Her sword and scabbard waited for her on the seat opposite.

Berith had already left, his meeting with Cernunnos the first of many, allowing for the transfer of power that would be his to wield as the master of life and death.

Naamah entered the room. "Lady Danu, I wish to fight with you," she said.

Danu considered her query but shook her head. "No."

Naamah opened her mouth to argue, but Danu stopped her. "I need a handmaiden, someone who will protect and oversee what I have built. Someone I can trust and rely on."

Shock resonated from Naamah. "But I'm a demon!"

Danu's smile left Naamah blinking. "Yes, but it doesn't preclude you from taking this role for me. I hope that once this battle is done, my future will be bright. Berith and I…" How did she even begin to explain that she desired a child? A family of her own, when it seemed like just yesterday, she'd considered giving in to the fade.

"Then I will protect what is yours."

"I have called my priestesses to the shrine. Protect them, Naamah, while they continue their rites. I will need all the power they can send at me once the battle begins."

"I will serve you with honour, Lady Danu." Naamah bowed deep, and Danu reached for the female.

"Thank you, Naamah. I feel like, when this is done, we may be friends as well as mistress and handmaiden." She clasped the demon's hand with her own. "I've never had a friend like this before. Berith was… He was my friend, but also my love. But you… you represent something else."

With that, Danu rose and gathered the belongings she'd need—the silver mask which would protect her face, the heavy shield, and her sword and scabbard—while she allowed her mind to settle to the task before her. Once she and the other warriors arrived at the designated battlegrounds, that's where they'd remain until the task was complete.

"Take care, Naamah. I will return, I hope, victorious." Then she stepped through the fold of space to emerge outside the house she knew as Padraic and Fenella's.

The building had changed a lot over the centuries, but she took a moment to scan the latest changes: the repointing of the brickwork, the new gardens, the drapes which kept out the chill of winter.

Before she could step up to the door, it opened and Padraic hovered. "It's time then?"

She nodded and followed him as he beckoned her within.

Cernunnos, the Watcher, was waiting for Berith as he walked up the hill.

"It's time, eh?" The god growled at him. "You've done well by

Lucifer, and after watching your careful stewardship, I can rest assured you'll assume my mantle and do it with due care and diligence."

Berith shook his head. "I never expected…"

"Aye, that's what made you a candidate. You didn't look to build an empire for yourself, you simply go about the task you were set." Cernunnos looked into the distance. "In life and death, there shouldn't be egos and self-interest, Berith. Now then, come inside and we'll talk a while."

Berith shifted. "I need to get back. The situation with Marrer…"

"Aye. She and that brother, for them it was ever about their interests. You know they didna know each other until you and Marrer were mated? Oh, she knew of his existence, but it was only after that he sought her out. Like flocks to like, some say. It was true in that case."

Berith considered the comment. "She knew of him, but no, I don't remember his existence before then."

"Aye. Zazrael was a minor general, and it was that which gave her the connections she needed, but you weren't aware of that. She hid truths from you from the beginning. Everything about her is a lie, Berith. Zazrael was raised by his father, they share only their mother, as you know. He was raised in the military, but he was not a strategic thinker. It's what ensured he never rose beyond that minor leadership position. But enough of that, today is about ensuring you understand this is a heavy responsibility."

Nodding, Berith cleared his throat. "I do. Life and death must never be easy decisions. It's something I've learned." He had learned through loss of Balala, but even now, that pain was receding, fading into a shadow so the memories of the good times were easier to remember.

"Aye. Balala and the child taught you much. It was my place to direct her to the next place." Everything except the sound of birdsong was silent as Berith digested Cernunnos' words. To be escorted by the God of Life and Death himself was an honour few knew.

"You took her yourself?" He whispered his question and waited, still and tense.

"Aye. She had her place in the prophecy and fulfilled it."

Cernunnos touched his shoulder, a gesture of understanding and solidarity. "She deserved my personal attention."

"Then I thank you, Cernunnos."

"Come. Come inside, and I'll show you the world I see, what you'll control soon enough. Then you can go, be with your true mate, Danu. She'll be needing you soon enough."

He followed the god inside the house, noting the walls of coarse wood, giving way to a contemporary room in hues of blue and white.

"What? You expected me to live in a hovel, boy? I've been here nine hundred years. Trust me, you get damned sick of draughts as you get older."

Berith snorted. "I still have my cavern."

"Maybe it's time to let go of that then, since I can't see Danu being comfortable in those surroundings. But come to the office, at the back of the house."

They entered a large room, computers beeping, but it was the far wall that caught Berith's attention. Suspended in the air, against the wall were baubles with faces on them, and interspersed were teardrops. They were ethereal. Not solid, and yet everything on them was clear, as if watching reality through a glass.

"This is my life's work, boy. Each bauble is a person whose life hangs in the balance. Their future unknown. I see them all, and I hear them all." He raised a hand, and one by one, Berith heard the sounds, beeping of machines and those weeping beside the objects of interest. Once Cernunnos flicked his hand, the sound ceased.

Berith could hear the sound of his own breathing, in and out, as he registered what he'd just seen and heard. The impact a drill in his mind. This is what he'd become soon. The knowledge was sobering. He advanced, closer to where they shone. "The teardrops, what are they?"

"Those are the innocent, unborn or just born. Some are ones who'll never be. Others will hang in the balance. I see them all, and if they fall, I catch them."

He considered the view before him. It was a weighty responsibility, but a question formed in his mind. "Can you see demons too?"

"You're thinking of Balala and the child?" Cernunnos frowned and sighed.

Berith nodded.

"No, I can't see demons or other paranormals and gods, goddesses. They are not guided by me, and many, particularly those of warrior factions, have no one to attend that aspect of their ending." Cernunnos pulled out two seats and indicated Berith should settle beside him. "I did see your child, because of its human mother. I watched as they came to their end. I was there for them."

Berith blinked. "Then I thank you."

He watched as one of the baubles darkened. Cernunnos reached out, whispered something inaudible, and the bauble dropped. The Watcher captured it in his hand and pressed a kiss to the surface before the bauble disappeared. Berith understood, without being told, that one of Cernunnos' charges had passed.

Silence filled the room as Berith considered what he'd just seen. The baubles and teardrops ranged in colour, the lightest and brightest to the top with the dark-edged ones moving down, seeming to organise themselves before Berith's gaze. The one thing they all had in common was they were the colours of the rainbow, from bright to dark. He would have expected more if Cernunnos was curating worldwide.

"Do you only care for this country?" Berith asked.

Cernunnos grinned. "If I were to take on more, I'd never finish, boy. So yes, this country is mine to protect and care for. Others do similar work in their countries. I know of no other that hasn't someone to fulfil the role I do."

Before, Berith had considered Cernunnos' task as overseeing, guiding the occasional soul. Now he knew better. He could understand the gravity of everything Cernunnos did. He reached out, but Cernunnos stayed his hand.

"No. If you touch it, that soul is lost before its time and they have no opportunity to recover," Cernunnos said. "I've seen souls so near to death make a dramatic discovery, so they must have every opportunity, without my interference." He smiled. "Some have memories of my watchfulness, others do not. I don't do it because of that, though, and there is an element of satisfaction in giving souls a quiet transition. Some go happily, the end of their suffering a kindness. Others go protesting, because they believed there was more to do or other chances. My people always do their best for those souls, Berith. We work closely, and once you take the mantle, they will do the same with you."

A thought occurred to Berith. "And when Danu is involved in a difficult delivery? Where there is a chance that mother or child may not survive?"

"Sometimes I'm there, beside her. Other times I see it from here and send one of my own to assist. But at the heart of it all, no one is ever truly alone when their time comes." Cernunnos touched his shoulder. "I was with Danu, Balala, and the child when that time came. Danu didn't face it alone, neither did your mate and child. They went in peace and love, Berith."

Danu settled on the rock in the middle of what would become the battlegrounds. The witches chanted quietly, ensuring humans couldn't accidentally stumble into the area once they'd begun.

Tonight, the vampires would arrive, and today the lycans expected to arrive and set up the physical encampment. At the edge of the fields, tents had been erected, and Padraic and Fenella, along with Grace and Luke, had already taken up residence in their chosen locations. Fenella and Padraic's children were being cared for by Michael, Padraic's closest friend, so they were safe, with a number of fae acting as their personal guards.

The fairies had taken their places in the trees, an effective early security system that she welcomed. They needed what little time remained to create a plan of action. Lucifer himself had already agreed to make an appearance, as had the Dagda and the rest of her siblings.

Whether they'd drawn in enough power yet remained to be seen, and while they'd reached out to other pantheons, those requests had been rebuffed.

A ripple moved through the air, and Danu rose, dusting her hands on the back of her pants as she waited. A vision appeared—Marrer, eyes burning with hatred. "I'll be seeing you soon, Danu. But this time, I'll have my army at my disposal."

"Indeed, it seems you've expended a lot of power, Marrer. Yet so far, you've not achieved any of the outcomes you desired."

The demon sneered. "I've come a long way since the first time I saw you."

Danu frowned. "I don't…"

"No, you don't. Even then you didn't see me. All you saw was a slave. Not someone who would change everything! Once I'm in control of the world, the likes of you will be wiped from memory." Her grin was feral, and a chill slid down Danu's spine. "The world will turn black, and all will bow down before me. On that day, you will bend to my will. You will serve me or die."

Danu straightened her shoulders. "I will not serve you, Marrer, because you will not win. Already your powers wane. Your grip on your armies is failing, and this is a single, last attempt of a sad creature to regain what was never yours." She leaned in. "You will pay for all your crimes, those who've died at your hand or your word. And remember, payment is due in full."

Marrer laughed, "You keep telling yourself you'll defeat me, because your only victory is in your mind. I'm stronger, more powerful, and my army is well-honed, ready to kill and dominate."

Fury ate at Danu, but she knew this for what it was, a chest-beating exercise designed to upset her. She wouldn't give Marrer the satisfaction, so she pasted a bored expression on her face and shrugged. "You keep telling yourself that, Marrer. If that's what makes you feel superior, but you know," she said and leaned closer to the vision, "Berith is mine, just as the victory will be. Now leave me." She waved her hand at the vision and waited until it dissipated, but not before she heard Marrer's roar of rage.

Scrubbing at her face, she considered what she now knew. Marrer hated her. A portion of the ire was hers and hers alone. She didn't remember ever seeing Marrer as a slave, but then again, the few caches of slaves who'd travelled the overworld were transported at night, only once or twice had she been able to see them. No memory stood out for her as she searched her mind.

"I need to concentrate," she told herself, spying Padraic weaving his way toward her.

"Lady Danu."

"Padraic, I think we're past that now."

He blinked, surprised. "You've always—"

"Yes. It was necessary to ensure no one got close enough, beforehand. Come, sit beside me. We have things to discuss."

He lowered himself to the grass beside her and sighed. "You've changed."

She smiled as the sun warmed her. "Perhaps, or maybe I've been keeping up barriers because I needed the distance to cope with the things I wanted and would never have."

"Berith?"

Danu turned to the leprechaun. "Yes, Berith. Marrer bespelled him and what was mine. He'd made his promise to me, then was snatched away. I considered the fade, Padraic, but now? Anyway, you've been a faithful servant and ally. After this is done, whichever way it goes, I release you from our agreement."

"You will release me?"

Her nod was firm. "A good leader knows when to let go. Besides, you have responsibilities. A family and those who follow you. Your stewardship is impeccable, and you've served me with honour. So yes, I will release you after this last battle."

"I always thought you a cold bitch, Danu. But this…?" He spread his hands.

"I was wrong it seems."

She laughed. "Well, I'm not sure I'd go quite so far as to call me sweet, but perhaps not quite the bitch you thought me. Though, there were times, I admit I teetered close."

His laugh was unfettered. "So, your plans after then?"

"I will retreat home for a while and concentrate on what I want." She sucked in a deep breath. "A family, if that's what Berith also wishes. And Naamah will need training, to be an effective handmaiden, though already she shows signs of excellent service."

"I have to say, I never expected that answer." Padraic laughed.

"Perhaps not, but I'm looking forward to a quiet life, for a while."

"Cressida will be here later today," he said. "We've organised onsite cabins to be delivered, and shutters for the inside to ensure their safety."

Danu nodded. "Will we be able to accommodate all onsite?"

"I hope so. We've a gazebo being erected today too, for meetings and for food. The witches are arranging the catering. They reckon several of the nymphs are extraordinary cooks, and Xavier is also bringing some of his own with him. One of them is a Mexican deity and her partner, a Russian fairy who also happens to have some other abilities."

"Oh," she said. "This world is indeed a marvellous place, and there are many more magickals than most humans perceive. Anyway, I noted that the relocatable bathrooms have already arrived. All we need now are musicians and the local humans will truly believe this is a private music party." The roadway in and out of the fields was bustling, but the only humans being admitted to the area were those who had been employed to deliver and erect items. "We need to make sure they're well clear of the area before this begins."

Already the tents were being put up, in small knots with braziers in the centre of each grouping, in case it turned chilly. The out-fields, owned by Padraic, were perfect for housing requirements.

"I've already got my crew double-checking the security. By the time Cressida and her lot arrive and the lycans, we'll be ready for Marrer."

"Don't be so sure," Danu cautioned. "We'll meet tonight and discuss what we know and strategy, but we can't afford to discount whatever she has up her sleeve. She has amassed thousands of demons."

Padraic grunted. "But they aren't necessarily committed to her cause, or even personal followers of hers. She controls the generals, it's true, but depending on how she's gained their fealty will be important in working out pressure points."

She nodded. Everything he said had merit. "So, bring those points with you tonight. Berith may have a better idea, and the Dagda is going to ask Ate to attend. She can't participate in the battle, but any intelligence she has will be welcomed."

"And Zazrael?"

She sighed. "Cernunnos will decide on what we do with him. I doubt we'll be able to gain anything, information wise, from him."

20

Berith found Danu in the gazebo, sitting at a table with the Dagda and Lucifer in human form, as he himself was.

"Grab some food," she told him as he sidled to the table. "Cressida and her crew will be here soon, and we'll want to plan our next move."

At her elbow was a dish, the aromatic scent wafting toward him. His stomach gurgled, and she laughed under her breath.

"I'll keep your seat," she said. and the smile she shot at him, warmed him.

He moved to where women were preparing meals and was offered fresh, crusty bread, a generous serving of stew, and a hot cup of coffee. Making his way back to Danu, he searched the crowd and noted there were about fifty so far using the facility.

Danu was halfway through her meal as he settled beside her. "A successful meeting?" she asked.

He nodded. "Yes. I'll tell you about it later." It wasn't that he was not wanting to share with the others his new designation, it was more he needed to work through what was in his brain, and he knew Danu would help him unpack what he'd learned.

"We'll have a full house tonight, and we'll be meeting with the leaders before midnight, hopefully. The plan is to use this area as a meeting place, and to pull together a strategy."

The Dagda speared him with a glance. "So, you're to be the new Cernunnos?"

Berith wanted to roll his eyes, but the man was part of Danu's family, so instead he nodded. "Yes, but I've much to learn. I will need to grow into the role, so for now, I'd rather not discuss it."

The man gave a short nod. "Fine."

Lucifer cleared his throat. "Danu, have you met with Padraic yet?"

Berith felt Danu stiffen beside him. "Yes. An initial meeting. There's more to discuss, but at least he understands my plans going forward."

"Have they changed?" queried the Dagda.

He felt Danu's hand quest for and take his. "Yes. Berith and I have an agreement. I won't be fading," she said.

He took a spoon of the stew and chewed, while she did the same. They needed time and space to talk about where their future was headed. Something they hadn't yet begun to plan together, and that would need to happen soon, if the query was anything to go by. At least, for now though, the Dagda seemed to understand their need for privacy on the matter and left the topic alone. For now, thought Berith, because in their world, little was unknown by those with power for long.

The sun had set by the time they'd finished their meal. "The days grow shorter," Danu said as she took his hand and led him to a large tent near the gazebo.

"Winter will be here soon enough," he agreed. Even now, there was the faint nip in the air. "We'll want all settled before it sets in."

She led him to the first tent, opened the flap, and he followed her within. He looked around, startled at the transformation of their accommodations. A warm fire in the centre, a large bed to the left, and a seating area on the other side. He quirked a brow at her.

"I made a few alterations," she said with a shy smile. "I wanted us to be comfortable. There's a bathroom to the back too. Not quite hotel quality, but better than needing to use the mobile bathrooms in the middle of the night."

"Indeed," he said, advancing on her slowly. "And the doorway?"

"I've a ward on the flap, no one can enter without our agreement." She gulped, "I used a hair from your human form to complete the spell."

He smiled. "You think I'm upset?"

Her lips quivered, somewhere between a smile and a grimace. "I didn't gain your agreement."

"I'm not angry," he whispered.

"Good," she said with a nod. "Because I have a wish and a need, Berith." She sidled closer and slid her hand over his chest. "Come with me," she crooned, reaching for his hand and leading him to the bed.

Her hand rose to the ties of her gown, and when it slipped to the floor, firelight dappled her exposed skin.

"Berith?"

He allowed himself a moment to watch with awe the beauty before him. Her body was firm, her breasts high and full, though mostly hidden from his gaze by her bra. Pretty though it was, with panels of lace, his fingers itched to remove it.

His hands didn't remain still, working at the clothes he wore. He could magic them away, but this perfect moment in time was about them, not their past or their abilities. He felt it in the air, the ripple of concealed need that radiated from her.

She slid off the bra and sighed, reaching for her panties, but though he was only partially unclothed now, he stilled her. "Wait," he muttered, feeling suddenly tongue-tied.

In this moment, so quiet and perfect, he too had a need.

"Danu, you've been in my life for so long, and until now, I've never truly understood what a gift you've given me. You've been with me during my times of grief, and times of pleasure. You protected what was mine, and when the time came, you stood by them. You're a trea-sure." He laid her soft hand against his chest. "I never truly understood the depths of your value, but I do now. If you'll have me as mate…"

He stopped because a single tear slid down her cheek. *She doesn't want me?*

Her fingers touched his lips. "All I've ever wanted is you, Berith. These words you're saying…" Another tear rolled down, shining in the firelight as she gulped. "I've only ever dreamed that one day you'd say them. You promised once, in the glade, that this day would come, then I lost you. Now you're here, and the moment… I'm overcome." She stared at him, her eyes emeralds shining so brightly. "Yes, I will mate with you, Berith. You're my heart and my soul."

He crushed her to him now, because suddenly everything came into focus; the moment when he'd told her the words, the way she'd looked so stricken when he'd gone to Marrer's arms… The memories rushed back at him.

"Berith?" Her whisper shook him to the core. "What's wrong?"

"I remember," he breathed, finally understanding the power of her pain and the depths of her forgiveness. "I remember it all, and I'm so sorry I did those things. I'm sorry I hurt you. The words don't seem enough."

"Shhh," she whispered. "Now is our time. What we have between us allows forgiveness. What has happened has been and gone. We look forward, Berith. We appreciate what we have." She reached up, cupped his cheek. He nuzzled her hand, sighing because love filled him, warmed him.

"I love you, Danu."

Pushing her hand away, he leaned closer and laid his lips to hers. Claiming her in the most basic way. The kiss was gentle, soft, and he infused everything into it. His love, hope, and dedication.

She gasped as he pulled away. "Tonight, we mate, my love. I want no more false starts between us."

"Tonight," she agreed and wordlessly removed the last of her clothing.

He removed what little remained of his own clothing, ignoring the puddled mess on the floor, because his total attention was given to her. His hand cupped her shoulder, drawing her close. "From this second on, I promise you my faithfulness, my love, and my soul. It is a gift I give you freely and is yours for time unending."

She blinked and he watched as she licked her lips, her cheeks betraying her nerves. "To you, I give my body and my soul. My heart belongs to no other, and I pledge, with free will, that my faithfulness will never end. To the end of eternity and beyond, I belong with you, and will support you, walk beside you, and be one with you."

The energy which had rippled through the room now glowed a blinding white light, signifying that their pledge was true and binding. "Come, love me, and be my mate," he whispered, lifting her to the softness of the bed, then climbed in after her.

He leaned in to kiss her and she met him halfway, her hands gripping his shoulders as her legs wound around his waist.

This kiss was wild, with tongues sliding against each other, until he tore himself away, inhaling unsteadily. "We have time, my love."

She giggled. "Perhaps, but we've wasted many years dancing around each other."

"I won't rush this," he told her, staring deeply into her eyes. "You deserve better."

She blinked away tears. "What I deserve has nothing to do with this, Berith. I love you, but tonight, it's just you and me. Now love me," she whispered, arching herself against him.

He ached for her, need flaring in the darkness as his hands slid down the length of her body, cupping her breasts before trailing his fingers over the sensitive tips. She gasped, and he smiled. "Sensitive, aren't you?"

He captured her waist, fingers and thumbs circling them and holding her still. "You've the body of a young girl," he muttered, and she choked back a laugh. Raising his head, he wordlessly asked why she reacted so.

"A girl does what she can to keep her boy interested," she giggled. "But I'm not sure of your interest right now," she bit out.

This time he laughed and positioned her. "Like this?"

"Oh yes," she whispered, and with a flexing of her legs, slid down his length. "This, forever."

He felt the pressure of her body, knew the moment she gave in to the pleasure. "My love, my heart. *My mate*," he intoned.

Her eyes widened, power making them shine like lights. "*My mate. Forever*." And the onslaught of magic drove them both to a frenzy, their bodies dancing and undulating until the precipice of pleasure loomed.

"Mate," he muttered again, feeling the sudden milking of her orgasm before letting go and following her into the place where only light and pleasure existed.

When Danu woke it was in the knowledge that she and Berith were now mates. It was a subtle difference about her, a buzzing of magic she'd not known in a long time, that was the first indication.

Climbing from the bed, she set the kettle to boil, knowing they'd both need to go into the night air, ahead of the first meeting with the massed army who'd come together to defeat Marrer. A hot coffee would bolster both their energy levels, of which they'd expended quite a bit, and she gave a small giggle at that thought. Add in the benefit of warding off the chill in the outside air.

She took her time, considering what had passed. "He remembers," she muttered. She didn't really know if that was a good thing or not, because he'd be able to tell when she'd realised, know of her pain. "I'd give anything for him not to feel that," she offered to the universe.

"Why?" Berith's question made her jump, and she gasped as the kettle she was holding in her hands splashed hot water over herself. "Did you hurt yourself?"

He was out of the bed, arm surrounding her and taking the kettle from her grasp before she could recognise his movement.

"Only a little," she muttered. "Let me finish…"

He shook his head and poured the water into the waiting mugs, then added the milk which waited on the tiny table nearby. "Why don't you want me to remember?" he asked, pressing the mug with now-finished coffee into her hand.

Biting her lip, she glanced down. "You've lived with pain for so long, I'd save you from more if I could."

"But that pain reminds me of what happened, how I acted. It reminds me that what we have, though deep, is also fragile. Something we have to nurture, as I have no wish to ever lose you again."

She blinked. "I'll be here by your side, Berith. I pledged my troth."

"Aye, and so did I," he said with a small smile. "You're glowing a little," he said, coming closer so he could inspect her form.

"It's the magic, taking time to settle into my bones once more. My body isn't used to having access to so much after a long time."

He frowned. "What do you mean?"

Shaking her head, she smiled. "We can discuss that later, but we should dress, and drink, then go to the gazebo. Cressida and her court are due to arrive anytime."

They dressed quickly in warmer clothing, and within minutes, they'd finished their drinks and headed for the gazebo, arm in arm.

When they reached the eatery, she stopped him and asked, "How do you wish to be acknowledged?" The question was on two fronts, and while she knew from her own perspective addressing him as her mate was one of the two answers she desired, it wasn't solely her decision.

As if he could read her mind, he turned to her and said, "You are my mate, as I am yours. As to my new role, perhaps we just use my name and see what comes from there, shall we?"

She gave a small nod and they entered together. A knot of others waited at the drinks area, and they walked over, while she was aware of the stares and interest in the eyes of those assembled.

Padraic loped toward her. "Made it official then?"

She blushed. "My mate, Berith. Padraic, I know you both know each other," she said and waited as the leprechaun extended his hand.

"Congratulations. It's good to have the original Danu back," he muttered to Berith, who took the proffered hand.

"It is my honour," Berith replied. "Now, will you make the intro-ductions? Some I know, but not all."

One by one, the crowd was introduced. Cressida was a beautiful blonde who brought her husband Daniel, also a vampire, along with Xavier and Hope, Javed and his vampire witch wife, who Danu had met before.

"This is the Lord of Lycans, Simon, and his mate, Niamh." Danu had met Niamh previously. She was a lycan who'd once been a fairy until a madman abducted her and amputated her wings. "You know Genevieve, of course, she's Padraic's daughter."

Danu smiled at the first leprechaun-lycan hybrid, before noting a lumbering man with a broad smile and an even broader accent when he said 'hello.' "Maxim is a healer, and a fairy and his wife is Pippa." Danu felt the ripple of magic surrounding the pair, and Padraic grinned. "Maxim is a Russian fairy who somehow found himself a minor deity, and Pippa herself is a goddess of sorts."

"You know such interesting people," Danu murmured, and Padraic barked laughter.

Padraic then waved forward one more couple. "And you've already met Grace and Luke, so you know their story."

Considering those who'd gathered, she frowned. "How do we make this work?" She whispered the words, but Berith's grip centred her sudden fears.

"We'll work it out, love. Have faith. It brought us back together," he whispered, and she nodded as the Dagda herded them to a set of tables which had been moved into a large square.

She and Berith took a centre on one side with Padraic, Fenella, Luke, and Grace flanking them. Cressida and her assembled crew filled one side by themselves, as did the lycan hybrid couples and those who'd travelled with them to bear arms. Another was filled with witches and wizards and an array of magic users. The last side was where Lucifer, Vinta, Dagda, and her siblings settled, spilling over to fill the empty spots on her and Berith's side.

"Now that we've all met and have an idea of our useful skills, we should share what we know. Berith, perhaps you might begin?"

Dagda, as a natural leader, opened the proceedings, and Danu was grateful. She might be a goddess, a warrior, and Berith's mate, but publicly speaking wasn't really a task she practiced or was comfortable with.

Berith cleared his throat. "Marrer is our primary foe. She's a demon, and for many years she had me believing she was my mate."

The silence at the table was palpable, and when the witch slid a cup of coffee before Danu, she nodded her thanks, without taking her eyes off those assembled.

"Using magic?" questioned Celina.

"Yes. She has no true magic of her own, or, I should say, a very small well. She took the goddess Ate as her prisoner and used her as a battery, which is, I believe, part of how she kept the ruse up."

Berith's answer caused a ripple of consternation around the table, and Danu rose to her feet, waiting until all eyes were on her. "She's been amassing magic by killing and absorbing other paranormals, including other demons. Berith was her mark as he was the librarian of the underworld," she explained.

"And you know this how?" Simon queried.

"We rescued Ate and have Zazrael as our prisoner," Danu answered, looking to the Dagda. "Will she be coming here?"

"Zeus has forbidden her involvement," he replied. "But she has written of her experiences, which will be made available to you after this initial meeting."

"And what do you need from us?" Cressida asked.

"Everyone here has played a part in overcoming a greater evil. We need your experience, your magic, and most of all, your support. Marrer is bigger than anything we've faced. We believe there is a well of magic beneath the ground and she'll need that to make her last effort to take control of humanity. We need to draw her out, bind her, then ultimately, the only surety is in destroying her." Lucifer spoke slowly and infused the words with the weight of their combined knowledge.

"So, no other gods or goddesses will be involved?" Cressida asked. "That seems rather short-sighted."

"No, they won't be involved. Most believe this is our problem and we must address it." Danu slid her hands into the pockets of her pants, feeling the perspiration of them. "Before you ask, they feel since the battle location will be here, it's our responsibility, and yes, they know that if we fail, there is significant danger to all." She shrugged, attempting to remain like she was at ease. Whether she pulled that off or not was anyone's guess at this point. "There are boundaries and many unwritten rules surrounding what we can and can't do and where we may or may not interfere. Even in America there are certain procedures we must adhere to, though they are laxer, given the circumstances." Some of the assemblage muttered at that, but she continued. "To be honest, we need to go beyond those boundaries, but until these dangers are cleared, there's no real will to prosecute the issue. But yes, it is something that requires addressing in the future."

Cressida settled into her seat, and her Life Partner Daniel leaned in and said something to her. She nodded, and Danu watched with interest the way the vampires seemed to discuss things amongst themselves. The way many nodded yet not a word was spoken told her they were discussing their thoughts telepathically.

"However, since we rescued Ate and took control of Zazrael, we also were able to remove one of her stronger personally aligned demons. She is weakening, and while she did gain access to the library —" Those assembled who didn't know of this, gasped. "—she is clearly not as strong as she was. But what she does have is a powerful army at her disposal. I can't say that they are all aligned personally, because I don't believe they are. What I will say though, is there is a likelihood that the cohesiveness of her factions is less than it was."

Lucifer cleared his throat. "My own people keeping an eye on the underworld have suggested that there are already problems, with generals planning to remove their forces beyond her control."

"She'll move with speed then," Berith muttered.

"Aye," said the Dagda. "Which is why we must form our plan now, execute it, and control the situation before she can strike."

Sipping coffee in the lounge area of their accommodations, Berith held Danu close. "I'm not sure I like this plan," he muttered.

She sighed and leaned back in his embrace. "I'm not keen, but we need to draw her out, and soon. Besides, you'll be there with me."

He grunted. Using Danu as bait wasn't great, but he understood the reasoning. Something else tugged at the edge of his mind. "Your magic seems more... bountiful."

Her laugh had him arching an eyebrow.

"What?" he asked.

"Naamah said something, before we sorted our mess out. She said I had a well, and could feel it, locked away. I didn't believe her, but I think she was right." Danu wriggled her fingers, and sparkles of light illuminated the inside of their haven. "I feel stronger and more in control. Like I found some kind of balance that I'd been missing for a long time." She giggled. "I feel young again."

The last vestiges of fear he'd tried to ignore fizzled out. "Because of us?"

She reached up and took his hand from where it lay on her shoulder. "I think so. I mean, part of my problem is that to recharge I need to be able to cycle the magic to my mate and back to me. Without that, I had no way..." She shook her head, and he wondered if she even understood her own power. The depths of it.

"Because of my promise?" The words squeezed out of him, still laden with pain.

"I don't know. It could be that my psyche locked away that magic, and when you left with Marrer, I lost control of it, or forgot how to access it. The rules of magic are fluid. Or at least mine, I guess."

He grunted. "Cernunnos is interesting," he said, changing the topic because he read her discomfort in their conversation.

"It was successful?"

He considered her question. "Yes, I guess it was. I learned much from him today, yet very little. His role... You were there, as was he, when Balala and the child passed. He told me."

"It wasn't that I was keeping it from you," she said slowly. "But you were in such pain. Would it have helped if I told you that?" She turned in his arms, looking at him, her gaze questioning.

"I don't know, Danu. But he guided them personally." He wasn't sure what to think, only felt a gratitude for both of them. The care they'd taken at such an important time.

She nodded.

"Thank you for your ministration," he said, the words slow and intentional.

"She was a woman at a point where only the best care and attention were necessary. I gave her my skill and…"

"Because you feel so deeply, it tells." He felt dull and slow as the fingers of weariness crept through him. "We should retire," he told her. "Tomorrow will be… difficult."

She smiled. "Today, really. If all goes to plan, this time tomorrow if it's not over we should be close."

"Take nothing for granted with Marrer. She's slippery."

Danu stood, placing her cup on the small table. "I know. And you're right, let's go to bed. To sleep," she added with a wan grin, and held out her hand.

He took it and followed her to the sleeping area, waited until she'd dressed herself in a warm nightgown before conjuring night attire for himself, and together, they climbed into the bed. They settled in, Danu in his arms.

"Thank you," she whispered.

"For what?"

"For being you. For loving me." She reached up, kissed him slowly on the lips, then with a smile curling at the corners of her mouth, she closed her eyes. "Now, we need to sleep."

He lay still, holding her in the night, listening to the sounds of the camp settling in, before he followed her to his own slumber.

Danu walked the field, looking for the centre of the magical well, as the final rays of the sun were dying away. The wind blew and her hair, ruthlessly contained in a braid, bumped against her back.

"Here," she told Berith. "This is where I need to be." She hunched down, touching the earth.

"If it's a magic well, why isn't it absorbing your power?" He sounded confused and reached down to help her up.

She cupped a hand over her brow, searching for something in the distance. Some sign of what was happening. Were the demons massing yet? They'd warded against human sight but allowed the demons to see them moving around the encampment. They would drop part of the warding soon, allowing the demons access through a single opening, but even that had to appear like it was a failure. Anything else would look too much like the trap they planned to spring.

"The land is tricky here," she answered Berith. "Padraic controls the land, so he controls the well. It's charged to whoever protects it, so our magic, light magic, I guess, is safe."

She felt the pull of the well, but it wasn't dragging at her, simply a buzz against her natural and personal shields. Padraic had walked the field earlier in the day with Fenella, Genevieve, and David, and as a family, they had renewed their connection to the earth beneath their feet.

Now, in the next field over, where the encampment lay, their army waited, shielded from sight until darkness, when the last of their comrades would emerge. But only after she and Berith prepared. Even now, the fairies informed them, the dark forces were gathering on the other side.

Danu took Berith's hand, and they headed away from the well. Soon enough they'd return for the final act. Soon enough, they'd know the side of the victor. She just hoped and prayed it was them.

"Marrer? They are massing at the site of the well. We must make a move soon, before they begin to use it to pull us in." Seetkri, the demon general, growled at her.

"Is it not warded?" she queried, feeding heavily, needing the boost of power. Since Berith had run off with the bitch goddess Danu, her grip on the magicks had waned. *I need more power. Without it, I will lose control of my army.*

"The wards are thinning and will fail soon. We can help that along," the general said, his eyes glinting.

She stopped her hand, partway to her mouth, blood running down her chin and fingers. "You can do that?"

He nodded.

She considered his words, the opportunity to stop Danu and Berith before they could strip more magic away from her. "Do it," she muttered. "Then come for me once it's done, and we'll end this."

Seetkri bowed low and backed away, leaving her with her bowl to feed some more.

Danu waited until Berith left before settling to the one task she'd promised herself she'd complete before the battle. In her hand was a tiny amulet, intricately fashioned in the shape of her personal motif: the triple spiral.

With great care, she pricked the tip of her finger with her silver dagger and allowed three small drops of blood to splash into the item. "For the love of mine, for the protection of mine, and for the shielding of mine. From danger, from magic, from death. So, I will," she chanted, before raising it to her lips. Her magic flowed into the tiny receptacle, and once it felt full, she kissed it. She'd give it to him, hung on a leather thong around his neck. "I'll not lose you to him again," she whispered, preparing it for his use.

Assured she'd completed this essential task, she placed it on the table by the fire and moved to dress. She did so with care this time, because, for all her bravado, she wasn't sure they'd be successful.

First came the black pants she favoured, silk woven by Brigantia, matched by the tunic top of the same magically infused silk. Next came her breastplate of silver, etched with her symbols: fish, water, and many more. The triple spiral took the place of pride in the centre. Her gloves were leather and fit perfectly. She slid the belt around her waist, the weight of sword and scabbard welcome.

She considered her face mask but shook her head and laid it on the bed. "Not today," she muttered. Instead, she conjured her shield, intricately wrought of silver and wood, with her triple spiral centred again, the strap sliding over her head and one shoulder.

Sliding her boots on, she sighed and closed her eyes, knowing the future was uncertain but taking the time to settle the nerves that quivered and jumped inside her.

The sounds of movement caught her attention, and her eyelids opened as she whirled. Berith was entering the tent.

"You're ready?" he asked.

She smiled. "Almost. But I have something for you."

Concern gnawed at her. Would he accept her gift?

She moved swiftly, grabbing the tiny item from the table. "Will you wear this? For me?" She opened her hand, extended to him, with the amulet there.

"Protection?" His brow quirked.

"Yes," she answered, silently urging him to take it. "I fashioned it myself. Please, for me and my peace of mind."

"It won't drain you?" He stared at her.

"No," she answered truthfully. "I've already charged it, so it shouldn't draw on me, unless you die," she whispered.

His hand covered hers. "I won't die. I'll be there to protect you, my love."

Tears stung her eyes. "Good. Wear it for me, under your armour."

They'd already agreed he'd take human form and wear the armour the Dagda, as a warrior god, had fashioned for him.

She waited for him to don the amulet then sucked in an unsteady breath. "I guess we're ready," she muttered and reached for his hand, and together they left the safety of their tent.

Marrer waited, the massing of her army not quite what she'd hoped for. "Where are the rest of the generals?"

Seetkri grimaced. "They've abandoned you, Marrer."

She seethed. *Abandoned me? I'll make them pay, once this is done!* "Once this is over, round up those who've run away like cowardly dogs. Bring them to me. I'll make an example of them." Her snarl had several of the demons backing up.

"Yes, Marrer," muttered Seetkri, his body tense and gaze narrowed.

"Now, an update…"

Berith glanced around, noting the numbers and types of paranormals. Many had come to support them. Lycans and vampires, witches, fairies, and even the notoriously unreliable fae. *Probably they came because if Padraic is lost, then the veil is open to Marrer's invasion.* They never did anything without self-interest high on the list. The leprechauns were there too, and the massed demons who'd joined them, led by Lucifer and Vinta at his right hand.

"Vinta is growing into his role," Danu whispered.

"He is. He's honest and fair and will do an excellent job as librarian, though I feel just a little responsible for the mess you said it was in."

"It's Marrer's fault. And it will be a good way for Vinta to stamp his authority on the collection."

The Dagda called them forward, explaining to the generals what their role would be, while outlining when and how each division would participate. The vampires waited to one side, not quite aloof, but neither part of the discussion. Cressida had already indicated their combined powers would be useful along with their physical ability to fight.

It was odd, in the past Berith had always known his job—that at the right hand of Lucifer—but today, he had one task… protect Danu.

Their intelligence had indicated that Marrer's hatred for Danu knew no bounds, and Berith agreed. He couldn't say when it began, but it was dangerous, and he'd stand between Marrer and Danu as required.

"We must draw them in. At the appointed time, once Danu and Berith are in place, the wards will look like they are failing on this corner of the field... The Dagda pointed to a board, showing the location. "The aim is to make the demons think they've breached it. But we must be patient, let them enter in numbers."

Voices muttered agreement as the Dagda completed his outlining of the plan.

By the end, silence reigned, while expectancy hung in the air, a palpable cloud.

A fairy entered and ran directly to the head of the vampires and whispered something. Cressida stepped forward. "It's time," she said, and they moved in silence, ready to take up their posts.

Berith took Danu's hand, and together they moved to the gate nearest them, ready to step onto the field. A bubble of concern grew with each step. At the entry, he stopped her, turned her to face him. "I love you, Danu."

As if understanding his fears, she nodded, eyes wide. "I love you too, Berith. I always have."

They took a moment, where he folded her into his arms. "You need to stay safe," he muttered against her hair.

He felt her nod. "I will, but so must you. We have a future before us, love, and maybe, one day, children. I'll do anything to protect that," she told him.

His heart squeezed in his chest.

"You must move," whispered Cressida, watching them.

Nodding, he released Danu, and together they entered the field.

21

A chilly wind blew, ruffling the few stray hairs that had escaped Danu's braid. She didn't look in the direction of the corner where the wards would drop, but stepped carefully toward the centre of the well, aware that Berith was stiff beside her.

The moonlight was dim, clouds obscuring their path, and the nip in the air reminded her that winter was approaching.

At the edge of the well, she stilled, bent down, and sent a tiny frisson of power into the soil. She released only enough to let it know she was present, but not enough to raise concern among those watching, especially the demons.

"What are you…?" Berith said.

"It's like a welcome, so any magic I use, or you use for that matter, the ground knows we are allies." She rose, a dandelion which grew around in her hand. She needed it to appear that she was seeking something. *Do nothing to arouse their suspicions.* The Dagda's warning echoed in her mind.

Three steps in and she stilled, raising her hands, the signal they'd agreed upon.

She felt the wards shiver, felt them drop, as if failing on the corner, and shuddered. Straightening her legs and spine, she prepared for the fight. She waited for the demons who'd soon flood the zone, her gaze averted.

Berith muttered, "First one," keeping her aware of their movements.

She moved, as if some incantation was taking place, all the while prepared for any attack that might come their way.

"Here they come," he said moments later.

A cry split the air, and now she turned, hand moving to her sword.

"Not yet," he muttered, though a brief glance told her he gripped the sabre he'd accepted from the Dagda.

Then there she was, striding across the field as if she owned it. Marrer.

Lights illuminated the night, and the demons stilled, uncertain as the massed vampire and lycan army, bolstered by leprechauns, other demons, and members of the pantheon swarmed.

The air was redolent with clangs and bangs as Marrer approached, her face tight while her eyes betrayed the madness of lust. Lust for power.

"I will kill you now, Danu of the Tuatha De Danaan!" She raised her hand, and a bolt of lightning flickered and arced.

Danu let loose a primal cry, grabbing her shield, and had it in hand before the connection could be made. She couldn't yet fight back, because she needed Marrer in the centre of the circle, then the witches would descend.

So instead, she stepped back, Berith sliding before her.

"You! Betrayer! Traitor!" Marrer screamed, spittle flying.

He swung, but a barrier encased Marrer, so the metal simply slid off, and with a wave of her hand, Berith was sent flying.

"Got him between your legs, did you? He was mine first!" Marrer screeched.

Danu smiled. "He was never yours. What you beguile was not yours to begin with," she taunted.

Berith was thrown backward. He landed at the feet of a burly demon general, one he knew well. Seetkri.

The bastard had been one of Marrer's first followers, likely hoping for a senior position in her new order should she win.

Berith rolled, just in time, as the wind from Seetkri's axe brushed against his shoulder.

"So, you chose sides? The wrong one," grunted the general.

"Never wrong. The one that keeps balance on this world," he retorted and reached for the sabre. It was missing.

He scrambled for an abandoned sword, snatched it up, and it arced through the air, missing the general. He stepped back lightly, aware that Danu was now on her own, and urgency filled him.

"Your head on a pike would be an excellent gift for my queen," muttered the demon.

"And yet, that's not going to happen," he answered.

Feet firm on the ground, he watched the axe, sought an opening, and swung fast and with all his might. The sword made contact, slicing true and deep. Blood spurted, and the look of surprise on the general's face gave Berith no satisfaction.

"What have you done?" The last words of the general were low, weak. He crumpled to the ground, and Berith whirled, looking for any sign of Danu.

He noted her at a distance, but between them, bodies writhed and grunted, moving like a bloody wave in the night.

Light filled the darkness, and he started to run.

Marrer lifted her hands again, and this time, Danu gripped her sword in one hand and shield in the other. The magic hit, hard. Danu panted and stepped back, well aware that she was still steps from where she needed to be, but putting up a good front was necessary.

The battle raging around them was forgotten as her concentration centred on the creature before her. "You've aged, Marrer. Magic that isn't yours does that to you." Danu laughed, infusing it with a sense of freedom she didn't feel. Inside, she quivered and quaked, because Berith hadn't returned. She couldn't avert her gaze though, because that would be an invitation to Marrer.

"All magic is mine!" The screech of madness betrayed Marrer.

"No, it isn't." Danu took another step, and Marrer followed, mirroring her.

"You had more magic than most. It's only fair that I take what I need," Marrer said, eyes narrow and sparking with hatred. Old blood, rivers of crust, adorned her chin, a chilling reminder that she'd killed and devoured those in her crusade.

"Killing and taking makes you a monster," Danu replied.

"I am a demon, monstrous is in my veins, just like I plan to do with you. Once this ground gives up its secrets."

Danu cocked her head. One last step. "You think?"

Now the streamers of light filled the night, and the witches who'd been cloaked entered the fray.

Marrer screamed, as with one voice, their chants began.

Danu advanced, sword held aloft. "Recant, Marrer. Be judged."

Her foe threw off the rictus that had captured her, and her voice boomed, "I am Marrer. I am the destroyer! I am the one who kills and devours. Submit unto me!"

Ripples of power filled the air, and Danu lunged, but Marrer danced away.

The chants of the witches, disrupted by the magic shockwave, now rose higher, as others joined them. The gods and goddesses swelling the ranks.

Marrer's face tightened, paled. "I will destroy you all!"

The ground rumbled beneath their feet, and for the first time, Danu had hope that they'd win the battle.

Whisps of energy eddied at her feet, and now, Marrer looked down, disbelief filling her features. "What have you done?"

Danu didn't dare drop her sword, not yet. She stood her ground. "This is a sacred place. It's a magic well, one that is attuned to those who control it. Earlier, when I touched it, I gave it a small charge of my own, so it would know who I am. What I am. I fed it."

Fighting against her magic bonds, Marrer twisted, hands extended, and sent a bolt of lightning toward her.

Danu's shield splintered, and she flew through the air. Pain ricocheted through her, but she forced herself upright and returned to where she'd made her stand. Wavering before the demon.

She needed to goad her, just enough so that the work of the witches wouldn't be constrained by her reaction to them. She just needed the demon to focus on her. "You will not win, Marrer." Danu sneered, stepping closer, as if unaffected by her previous attack. "You will be bound."

As if it broke through the wall of restraint, Marrer sent blast after blast at her, and Danu tried to dodge and weave, but enough reached her, each weaker than the last but still enough to inflict damage.

Through watery eyes and limping, sword tightly gripped in her hand, she approached the demon.

Hands grabbed her, warm, firm yet caring. "Danu, stop," Berith whispered, his breath a caress. "It's done."

The words stilled her. "Marrer?"

"The witches and your siblings have done their job. She is bound."

She dropped to the ground, every part of her body screaming in agony. "I'm... a little banged up," she muttered.

"Yes, you are, but her army is scattered. Ours won the day, love. But now, you need medical attention."

"But... Marrer?"

"The binding will hold her until you are able to participate in her judgement, love. Look, here comes Lucifer now, bringing the healers. Just stay still.

Berith carried Danu to the tent, noting the pallor of her skin and the blood that seeped through her clothing. He himself was largely unharmed, and he knew with a bone-deep certainty it was the amulet.

He felt the heat of it against his skin, like a lover's caress.

Terror filled him, because what if something Marrer had hit her with was a mortal wound?

Once inside, he laid her on the bed, and the healers streamed in behind him. They surrounded the bed, one turning toward him and muttering, "You should step back so we can work."

He watched, a feeling of helplessness almost overwhelming.

A hand touched his shoulder and he turned. Lucifer.

"What?"

Cernunnos appeared at the tent flap, and his heart froze. "Not her," he begged.

"Nay, I'm not here for her. Her wounds are not serious, but there are many on the field, and I am here for them."

He sagged. "Thank you," he muttered.

"I brought you this, though. It seemed the right time." Cernunnos pushed something into his hands. A letter.

"What?"

"From Balala," Cernunnos murmured before leaving.

Lucifer steered him toward the seating area, as if understanding he wasn't prepared to leave Danu.

"You should read it," Lucifer told him.

He unfurled the letter, hands trembling.

My dearest Berith,
These are my last words to you, and I've requested Cernunnos to deliver them when the time is right.
I know of the prophecy that one day you and Danu will be one. You will do what must be long after I am gone.
I am, and have always been, proud of you and loved you. Danu loves you and always has too. I am proud to have called her friend and have her stand by me, just as it is the measure of who you are, that we both know your worth.
When the time comes, love her with all your heart, knowing that I know she stepped aside for me, as I now do for her. Cherish her forever, my love.
Balala

His hands shook and tears escaped, obscuring his vision.

Danu rose, still aching but much improved after last night's battle. "I'm pleased they waited until tonight for the judgement," she muttered to Berith as he settled her into the chair at the centre of the proceedings, then took the one beside her.

No one turned a hair as he took her hand, Cernunnos hovering behind. "We're just pleased you're upright enough for this," her sibling, Rhiannon, murmured.

Marrer was dragged in, her generals having already been dealt with by Lucifer, who'd released Lucifuge Rofocale from his prison cell and demanded he pass immediate sentence on them.

Danu didn't ask what their sentence was, because she had a fair suspicion already.

Marrer screamed and squirmed as she was dragged forward, those in attendance sitting in rows, watching with interest what would come to pass.

The Dagda rose, as did Lucifer, who took the lead for now. "Marrer, you are charged with wilful destruction of the demon realm, the slaughter of innocents, and an attempt to circumvent the balance of light and dark in the world."

"So?" She spat at those gathered. "It was mine! My right to challenge for the power."

The Dagda cleared his throat. "The right to challenge does not extend to other paranormals, or the earth, only those of your kind."

"I will be a god!" Marrer bellowed, her dark skin turning darker in her fury as blood filled vessels in her face and neck. "I will dominate, and all will bow before me!"

Lucifer sighed. "You show no remorse."

"Why should I? Let me go or you'll regret your actions."

Lucifer and the Dagda turned to those gathered. The Dagda cleared his throat. "It is our right and place to pass the judgement. If she is found guilty, there can only be one sentence." With a bow, he took his seat and waited for Lucifer to make his comments, but he stepped up to Berith.

"You will be Cernunnos, the God of Life and Death. It is right that you should be the final determiner."

Danu felt the clenching of his hand beneath hers as he rose, turned first to her then her brother, Cernunnos. "It should be yours by right," he muttered.

Cernunnos shook his head. "It is your first act, be wise and thoughtful," he added.

Berith nodded and turned to Danu. "You agree?"

She knew his thoughts and nodded. "I do."

He moved slowly with the grace he'd always possessed and stood before Marrer. "As my first act, replacing Cernunnos, I pass judgement on you. Finding you guilty of all you've been charged with and more. There can only be one outcome, as the Dagda has said. You will be taken to the well, where your destruction will be enacted. Make it swift, make it as painless as possible," he told the witches and pantheon.

A sound tolled, rolling over the valley around them.

Danu sat up, knowing what the sound implied. She rose, took his hand, and they led the others from the shelter into the field, aware that Marrer, still screeching and threatening those in attendance, was following.

"What is that sound?" Berith asked.

She glanced at him. "It is the alert that a passing is happening in our homeworld. Once a new day dawns, a new monarch is to be crowned."

He frowned. "What do you mean?"

She turned as they took up their position in front of the well. "I'll explain later, but it's part of why we were expelled from our homeworld."

He accepted her answer, then turned as the execution party assembled.

The witches each touched Marrer as they filed by her, and Danu knew it was to ensure that during the next moments, she could not escape her bonds.

Lucifer stepped up to the well and pushed Marrer down, so she lay upon the ground. Padraic squatted in front of the demon, sinking his hands into the dirt. "Let it begin," he said, and the witches began their chants, as Celina sprinkled a powder over the demon who panted and writhed on the ground.

A fairy placed a flower upon Marrer. "The earth is a vessel, absorbing light and dark. In this place, at this time, absorb that which we offer."

Cressida placed a coin on Marrer. "It is in this time and place we offer our thanks to the earth which sustains us," she said, then kneeled next to the fairy.

Simon, the lycan, a piece of raw meat in his hands also offered it, "To the world which feeds us, we offer thanks."

And lastly, Danu rose. In her hands she carried a piece of parchment. "To this world, which has taught us of love and loss, we offer our undying thanks."

Then she returned to Berith who enclosed her in his arms.

The glow on the ground rose to become a wall, and beams of light illuminated the darkness.

Then as quickly as it came, the light was gone, as was Marrer.

Padraic sighed. "The earth has taken her, absorbed her, and her power released to the universe. It is done."

Berith waited with a hot drink in his hands as Danu turned from the others and made her way slowly toward him, her smile soft. He passed the drink to her and waited as she settled herself on the seat and sipped. The others in the tent were drifting into groups.

"Thank you," she whispered.

"It's nothing," he insisted, and she smiled.

"I promised you an explanation. So, let me see, where do I even begin?" Her hair was loose tonight, a red curtain, and her fingers toyed with a curl. "Before we came here, my siblings were… let's say, not outcasts, but vocal against our leader. He was vain and power hungry. A little like Marrer."

He waited, aware that she was struggling to tell him something she'd kept secret for so long.

"He had a plan, wanting a power that wasn't his to begin with. He wanted to be more important than the sun. It was his idea to become the god of the universe, to absorb the sun, so the only heat and light was his. He believed that would make him a supreme god, and even his father would owe him fealty."

Berith cocked his head. "That sounds oddly megalomaniacal."

She snorted. "Just a little. So we came together, planned to warn his father, the senior god, or father, of our world. But when we arrived, he'd already been warned we were coming, someone had made a deal with him, and in thanks for the warning, we were removed from the realm as threats to the new order."

"And I hesitate to guess he, the son, was defeated?" Berith queried, taking her hand in his.

She nodded. "Yes, but the father couldn't remove our powers, just closed the gateway to our home, so we can't return once we were evicted. That's how we ended up here. Outcasts who've made their own place and homes."

"And that's a secret because…?"

She screwed up her nose. "Knowledge of the otherworld is forbidden to those who are not directly associated. It was one of the rules we agreed to. We keep the secrets, and we are left in peace."

"The bell?"

"The father has passed. We are no longer bound to the agreement, and I suppose we could return but…" She shrugged. "I doubt any of us will. We've built lives and families here. This is now our home."

Berith smiled. "Good. Now, let's go home."

She laughed. "Not yet. There are a few loose ends to tie up, but soon."

EPILOGUE

Berith waited by the door. Danu had bustled out earlier and was due to return any time now. Naamah, now Danu's senior handmaiden, had prepared a meal for them, then left, a delivery to oversee.

In the time since they'd mated, much had changed. For the better.

In his office, all was well. The baubles hung, as did the teardrops, which were there waiting for him to tend, and Cernunnos would be by later to spell him, so they could spend time together.

Berith glanced out at the meadow surrounding Danu's—and now his—home.

"It was a hard winter," Lucifer said, and Berith turned quickly.

"I didn't know you were planning on dropping by."

"Only for a short visit this time. Vinta sends his best and said that all is well in the library, and the minions who've joined him are settled in well."

Berith nodded. "You don't just drop in though," he muttered.

Lucifer laughed. "No, I don't. I wanted to bring you news."

Cocking his head to one side, he waited. But Lucifer was in a strange mood. "What?"

"I've taken a mate." Lucifer frowned. "I don't quite know how it happened. One day she turned up, then she stayed. And no, there's no amulets or magic spells involved. She's… I'd like you to meet her. She's a descendant of Balala's sister."

He felt a smile on his face. "Then I'm very happy for you. And yes, Danu and I would love to meet her."

Lucifer's face smoothed over, telling Berith how worried he'd been. "Then I shall leave you, and we'll settle a date and place. Maybe in your world?"

Berith nodded, and Lucifer disappeared just as Danu entered the house, her face flushed and eyes sparkling. The basket in her arms was filled with produce, and he hurried over to take it from her. "You're not supposed to be carrying heavy loads," he reminded her, glancing at her distended abdomen.

"I can carry a basket of produce." She laughed, placing her hand against her bump and smiling. "She's kicking. Here, feel."

He placed the basket on the table and slid his hand over the babe hidden within her body. "She's getting ready," he muttered.

"Aye, that she is."

He pulled Danu into his arms. "Lucifer was just here. He's taken a mate."

"Oh really? That's wonderful news."

"A descendant of Balala's sister," he offered. waiting for her reaction.

She turned in his arms to face him. "Does that worry you?" Her fingers traced the lines of his face.

"No. All I feel is pleasure for him and her."

"Then I'm happy. Now, come help me make dinner. Cernunnos will be here soon, then we can leave. Padraic and Fenella and the children are waiting for us. I don't want to be late."

"Never that," he muttered.

His heart was full. He'd evolved and changed, built a good life and was truly happy. He had the woman he loved and a child on the way. His memories were his own, and they had a long and joyful future ahead of them.

The End

THE BLOOD BRIDE BY IMOGENE NIX

Hope just wants to be an ordinary nestling. She went to college and escaped, but now she's back and there's a secret everyone is keeping from her.

Xavier is the new master of the nest, ready to welcome home the daughter of the house who he has never met. He's unprepared for the woman who steals his breath and enchants him.

Now Hope and Xavier must fight for lives and those of the innocents. After all, it is only by overcoming the rogues that they will have a chance of a timeless future together. But will it be in time?

PROLOGUE

As silence descended on the house, the shadows grew—dark grays and blacks that bled into each other. First one figure then another broke away, making a run toward the house. Silent as the grave, they moved swiftly over dew-slicked grass. Then they stopped still. Waiting. Not a movement betrayed them until a signal propelled them back into action and they started crawling upwards. The walls damp coating no barrier to the intruders that ascended in the darkness.

The sound of each window breaking shattered the quiet—the figures were inside. Screams echoed through the night. Yet, in this area of large estates, heavy with noise-absorbing shrubbery, no one could hear those within. The blood-curdling screams went on and on before finally dying away.

Just one sound echoed through the night: The sobbing of a child.

The front door opened and figures trooped out—ghostly specters against an inky night sky, broken by a single outline. A child in white, carried at the center of the pack.

No sound broke the silence as they moved toward the trees surrounded the house.

Flames now licked at the manor: A deathly glow of oily smoke rising.

All that remained was a single person—wrapped in a cape of midnight blue beyond the house—watching them melt away.

Jemima moved toward the burning structure, breaking into a run as she breached the threshold. Vainly she attempted to enter, but the heat drove her back.

Now dashing tears from her face, she raced across the graveled driveway toward the gates, where the guardhouse was located. No sign of life existed within the building and some instinct of survival slowed her pace to a careful creep. Out of breath and heaving from exertion, she nervously checked within.

Small puffs of white vapor colored the glass. She darted from one window to another. Her cloak drawn tightly around her body, hoping it would camouflage her from sight.

Satisfied, Jemima entered through the heavy, wooden front door and moved toward the phone she spied on the floor. Her eyes darting here and there she dialed, listening to the rotary motor as it returned to the proper position. Time was short and if *they* came back, she needed to have shared the message.

The phone rang once. Twice. With a brrping sound it connected.

"Hello?" A male answered and she felt a warm flush of relief at the voice. A voice she knew well.

"The manor has been breached. The girl child taken." The words erupted and her hand trembled.

"On our way." The click of the receiver being replaced echoed loudly in the stillness of the room.

Copper. She smelled copper.

Her stomach soured, knowing it meant more deaths. Jemima looked around for the gun—a gun with deadly, holy water-infused copper bullets—she knew was hidden somewhere in the room. A gun she couldn't find. *No divine intervention exists here,* she thought.

Hopefully *they* didn't remain. Feeding. If they were still here, that's what they would be doing. She found a corner and scrunched down, hiding from sight.

Crouched low, she tried to stay as still as possible, listening for sounds of the vehicles she knew would be coming. She dug her fingers into the flesh of her arms; remaining aware enough to stop before drawing blood. That would surely bring them out. Jemima dragged the cloak around her to capture the warmth, yet there was little to be found.

The sounds of engines roused her from the corner of the room. Jemima inched toward the window, the lead of the old glass distorting her view, hearing raised voices she knew Mistress Cressida had arrived.

Jemima retreated. Remained hidden from the woman because if she knew, all may well be lost. From the shadowed room she listened to the conversation...

"It smells like Estersham." The Mistress' eyes closed. "If it is, we have a problem." She turned once more, her face set and eyes now glacial in intensity. "James?"

The man nodded as if he knew what was to come.

"If I take those steps, I cannot return. Another must stand in my place." Her voice hardened while her eyes glittered in the dim light, piercing in their intensity.

Then the Mistress' voice called out in the near silence. "You and yours have been my loyal servants for so many years. I took an oath to protect you long ago. I renewed it with marriage and births, over and over. Now, my home and yours have been breached and this child taken from us. The girl child, who will be the hope and salvation of our kind, was ripped from the bosom of our nest. I will repay your loyalty and I will get her back." The words of power rippled in the night and licked at Jemima's skin.

Available in Ebook
books2read.com/BloodBride-Nix

Direct Autographed Copy
https://www.imogenenix.net/BloodBride

THE RESET

A zombie apocalypse is here, but figuring out how to survive in the immediate aftermath is only the first step.

Elaine is just an ordinary woman, but when the apocalypse occurs, she must find a way to survive in an increasingly hostile world. Enter Liam, the policeman who saves her at their first meeting and provides assistance as they try to cope with the zombie outbreak brought about by an unknown infection that's spreading out of control.

Together they form a community, trying to save as many lives as they can, a place where people can be safe. Even in the throes of disaster though, emotions creep up, taking both of them by surprise. Who knows? They might just get their happy ever after…if they can survive.

Elaine's fingers curled over the radio, her heart stuttering with fright.

"Officials are unable to determine the cause of the illness breaking out all over the city, but urge calm. If you are cornered by the infected, seek safety. Should you be bitten, seek medical attention immediately."

Her fingers fluttered against her lips. The dirge rose, long moans as those infected, their skin turning a deep grayish green and their eyes milky white, howled outside the office. Elaine pushed the curtain aside once more and glanced through the glass. The collection had grown, their faces slack yet eerily aware that she remained inside.

"I don't know what to do." She turned back to watch as her boss, William Eckerman, rocked in his seat. "I mean, we've been holed up here for over two days. There's no food in the kitchenette, the toilet is overflowing, and we can't stay here, otherwise we'll die." The jitter of her stomach warned her that panic was rising up, about to overwhelm her.

"Elaine, relax. It's just a precautionary measure. The police will come and…"

"The police have indicated that they are overwhelmed. Military forces are on the way, but communications are hampered by the…by the walking dead converging on sites with power. In the latest update, the government is ceasing all non-urgent tasks. They're recommending that you hunker down and hope you can ride it out. Resources are limited, and it's suggested that, if possible, you should stock up and find a safe location in which to secure yourself." The announcer's voice shook.

"See? They're saying we need to find a secure location, stock up, and hide. Mr. Eckerman, we can't stay here." The urge to flee coursed through her veins like an exploding freight train. "We have to go to our homes. Be with our families."

He flicked invisible specks of lint from his immaculate sleeves and rocked again in the seat. "Well, Elaine, I think, given your current level of excitation, you should certainly go home."

She frowned at the cool tone. "Uhhh, Mr. Eckerman?" "Yes?"

"Mr. Eckerman—"

"When this is over, I'll give you an excellent reference for the four years of service. It's sad that something has overset you to the point where completing your work is no longer your priority. I understand it is probably time to expand your employment horizon."

As she stood there listening to the drivel he was spouting, growing anger warred with her terror. "Mr. Eckerman..."

"Go on and get your things together. It's best you go directly home."

She shuffled to her desk, shock assaulting her as she gathered the few personal items she'd stashed. The photo of her parents, the Mickey Mouse cup she'd bought at a major attraction. The hairbrush and small clutch of cosmetics joined the rest of her belongings, then Elaine straightened, turned, and headed for the door.

"Aren't you forgetting something?" Mr. Eckerman held out his hand, and she blinked. "Umm, what?"

"Keys."

She blinked again then made an 'O' with her mouth. "I forgot them when I came in. I'll have to drop them off once everything is done."

He snarled and opened the door. "Go on then. I want them back here as soon as the situation is cleared."

She looked outside, glad he'd insisted on staff using the back door, which was protected by the security fencing and remote-controlled roller door. She hurried to her vehicle, pleased it was older and heavier, sure it would protect her until she reached home.

Leaving the building was scarier than she expected. As she drove the short distance she constantly glanced around, seeing small huddles here and there of those who were infected. Each time they lurched in her direction she panted, heartrate increasing, adrenaline spiking until she was past them.

Turning onto her street left her amazed. Smoking wrecks of cars littered the street, and several gray-skinned individuals loitered. She drove carefully, hoping she could make it home without being waylaid.

When she reached her house she swung in to park on the road, thinking she'd have plenty of time to get in the house without any of the walkers in the way. She found the key for the front door, checked the rearview mirror to make sure none of the infected were close by, then got out of the car. Slamming the car door shut, she engaged the locks and sprinted to her front door.

Fighting the jamb until the door eased open, Elaine slid within and pushed the door shut. The tiny house on the outskirts of town she shared with her best friend had a deserted feel to it.

"Emily?" Once sure the door was securely latched she hurried up the hall, calling her friend's name. Every door she opened and peered inside was empty, and at the end of ten fruitless minutes she slumped down in a kitchen chair.

Liam wasn't sure what to do. The supermarket was empty, and shelves of food were scattered on the floor as he picked his way along the aisles.

"They said to lay in supplies then hunker down." He glanced at the phone in his hand. "They didn't say to break into the supermarket though." Ramon, his half-brother, snickered into the camera of the phone, and Liam shrugged.

They'd flown into Canberra three days ago and settled into the tiny B-and-B on the edge of this township. The location seemed great, only a few miles from Parliament House. It was close to the venue of the three-day conference he was attending on policing in emergency situations. Ramon had come because he'd concluded his last contract in an African country with a bubonic plague epidemic and was at a loose end.

No one could have expected something like this outbreak to occur though, and food was a priority. Liam had insisted Ramon stay at the B-and-B. Having a brother who was an epidemiologist and infection prevention specialist meant he might be called upon by the authorities for assistance, and they couldn't afford for him to be infected by the virus.

"Okay, I'll see what I can find and get back there as quickly as I can." Liam disconnected the call and turned to scan the shelves. "Long-life milk, because it will be good for at least a year on the shelf, sugar, coffee. Bottled water. Some powdered milk as well." He thrust them into the trolley and moved as quickly as he could toward the end of the aisle.

A groan stilled him. He'd already seen the results of those infected, the way they set upon victims, the dripping, bloody teeth. If that moan was anything to go by, he was no longer alone in the shop.

"Get back!" The startled words of a woman almost had him jumping.

"Hello?" He cursed inwardly for now making himself a target as the sound of shambling footsteps echoed, moving in his direction.

"He's heading your way!" the woman yelled as the gray man turned the corner, eyes blank, mouth slack through dripping trails of scarlet. The outstretched hands moved toward him. He didn't have anything on him that would be considered a weapon and cursed that decision. The paperwork for going armed in public—something the department had been cracking down on lately—would have been worth it after all.

The creature extended its arms and gave an "uhhh" sound, and he pondered for a moment whether there was some way to disable it. The thought came and went when the woman screamed and a second and third shuffler made its way in his direction.

The handle of the trolley was just in reach and he tugged it backward, braced his legs, then ran in the direction of the shuffler. The trolley hit the creature in the chest, and it went down, legs and arms waving frantically until it rolled. Now the sound that emanated from its mouth became more of a growl of fury.

He reached out, his hand curling around the nearest can. Saying a silent prayer, he aimed and threw. The crack of heavy metal on bone and the spray of blood as the man went down without a whimper gave him momentary pleasure, but not before the woman from the next aisle scurried around to him.

"There's two more," she screamed.

He didn't glance at her, merely reached up, grabbed another tomato soup can, and lobbed. It hit without the power to cease the onward march.

"Dammit!"

"I've... There's some kitchen string here. Would that help?"

He turned briefly and acknowledged the beautiful, curvy, red-haired woman thrusting the plastic-wrapped item at him, but he shook his head as they stumbled backward.

"We're going to need something a little more useful." He considered what might be here in this tiny store as the woman disappeared before returning with two long, metal-headed rakes. "What about these?" she asked.

He laughed, grabbed one out of her hands as the walkers came within reach, and thwacked it down hard on the head of the nearest one. The rake dropped with a thud and rolled under the shelving unit.

She made a sound, rather like a moan, and turned away as he snatched the other implement and used it to push the other shuffler back.

This time he lined up the male, sidestepped its attempt at grabbing him, then swung this new rake like a bat. The infected individual fell to the floor, and he brought the rake down on its head. She turned and retched while he waited.

"They're... Those were humans! Why did you—"

"No, they aren't humans anymore. They were zombies, and they'll kill you as soon as look at you. Now grab what you need so we can get out of here."

He glanced down one last time at the remains he'd left on the floor. He felt bad about what he'd had to do, but sugarcoating the truth wouldn't make it any better. The only thing they could do was stock up and get back to safety.

He threw tins and jugs into the trolley, along with frozen items, which he was sure would only be available for a little while longer. He also tossed in other essentials such as toilet rolls. He noted that the woman, tears flowing down her cheeks, followed his lead.

Then, with both trolleys full, they left the store and headed to the carpark. This was the danger time. He pulled out his cellphone and dialed Ramon. "Hey, I've got a full load and I'm heading in."

"Good, 'cause I'm hungry and the radio is just repeating what we already know."

He turned to the woman. "Will you be all right to get home?"

She sniffled inelegantly and nodded. "I'm just over the road there." She pointed to the

tiny cottage beside the B-and-B residence where he was staying, and he laughed. When she glanced at him, he sobered. "I'm right next door."

"Oh."

Available from Love Books Publishing
https://books2read.com/Reset

Direct Autographed Copy
https://imogenenix.net/product/the-reset/

A VERY MERRY WIDOW

A Very Merry Widow

Louisa thought she'd made the right choice. Jeremy had been the man she'd loved, but he wasn't who she thought he was. After he dies in a horse riding accident, she wants more. Not another husband, but perhaps a lover who'd fulfilled her needs while she raised her daughters.

Albert never expected to return to England, let alone to take up the family seat or the title of Earl of Conney. Yet here he was, returning from the wilds of Australia, with his friend, Frederick. A convicted felon. He'd sworn to himself if he was going to assume the title, he'd use the influence that went with it to clear his friends name. Brothers-in-law, Langdon Devereaux and Aeddan Fitzsimmons are the connections he needs, and they bring him into the contact with Louisa Lavenwood, a beautiful and aloof widow with two gorgeous but young daughters.

But she has a dark secret, and this unwilling hero feels the need to save her. Along the way passion explodes and they're helplessly lost in its thrall; if only they can overcome the danger, then perhaps more than passion lies in their future.

Louisa watched as the casket containing the body of her husband, Jeremy, was lowered into the ground. His coffin of dark oak and silver fittings shone in the weak daylight, and emotional numbness filled her senses. The fog of the morning had lifted a little, but the cold seeped into her bones as she dragged the heavy, black shawl close around her shaking body. The sounds of weeping from her mother-in-law beside her had been her companion since the accident. Now with the funeral passed, there was only the wake left to survive, then she could consider what came next. Where her future lay.

Her hand, clenched in a black kid glove, was slightly obscured by the black mourning veil she wore as she wiped at her cheek, hoping they'd not look too closely and know. Black would be the only colour she'd wear for a year because convention dictated it, followed by another year of grey, half-mourning. She hated knowing that she would be restricted again.

The bombazine of her gown, heavy and stiff, dragged at her body as her mind whirled with everything and nothing.

Since Jeremy's death, so many emotions had enveloped Louisa, but she'd held them tight within her breast.

Fury that he'd been so stupid as to be riding in a storm.

Grief that the man she'd loved had been taken from her.

But most of all, *betrayal*, because she knew who he'd been with.

There was more, she just knew it, but hadn't yet had time to enquire of her family's man of business. A man like Jeremy, one who'd lied to her face, who'd strayed just days before she gave birth... The truth was coming out, and she welcomed it with a vicious stab of honesty.

A storm was brewing—rage growing—and if *her ladyship* thought she'd simply keep quiet and sweet, she was in for a startling awakening. The roiling fury had grown in the last three days, and she promised herself that soon, she'd release the poison and begin to heal.

As soon as the requirements of widowhood were done, Louisa told herself as her eyes stung.

Exhaustion dragged at her weary mind.

She barely heard the words of the minister, committing her husband's remains to the ground.

All she knew was, with a child and a newborn babe, she was a widow. Alone in a man's world.

A hand reached out, took hers. *Elspeth*. Both her sisters, Isabelle and Elspeth and their husbands had made the trek back to the family home to support her when she needed them most. Men who were well-born. Men who she hoped would protect her from her mother-in-law's vicious tongue. Men who would protect her while she learned what she needed to know and while she decided what her future would look like.

Now wasn't the time to explain. There hadn't been time to do so before the funeral, but once Jeremy's family left, her sisters and brothers-in-law would hear all. It wouldn't be pretty, but she'd need their support. To make plans. Not just for herself but also her daughters.

Dirt was pressed into her hands, and she glanced down at it. "You need to throw it," Elspeth muttered.

She followed the instruction without a word, crouching down to ensure it thudded on the lid of the casket. Then she stayed there for a moment, silently considering. Finally, she rose.

The minister extended his hands. "I'm so very sorry for your loss."

She whispered something. It was probably the right words, but right now, she held tight to her control, the only thing that had bolstered her for the last few days. Ever since learning of Jeremy's betrayal and death.

At the gate, the carriages waited, one for her and her sisters. Their husbands would ride beside the jet-black conveyance. Another waited for Jeremy's grieving parents, and the rest of the family who'd attended had arranged their own transport.

Walking to the vehicle, silence echoed, apart from the cry of a crow. The sound crass and discordant.

Awareness that his family followed was cloying. Freedom was what Louisa craved most right now. Her sisters would surely see that and understand.

It was only once they were settled inside the carriage and it was moving that she took their hands. "Thank you for coming, sisters. We must talk. But after his family leaves." Her voice sounded scratchy from the night before, sobbing into the pillow that still faintly echoed the scent of Jeremy.

"Of course we would come." Isabelle patted her hands.

"You needed us, so we're here," Elspeth offered.

Looking at her sisters, both married with their own children, and returned to England, she wondered if she'd been too young. Too innocent. Too unaware when she'd accepted Jeremy. Thoughts of that day, the gown she'd worn, and the flush of success had gulled her into accepting a flawed man.

Her sisters had been initially concerned but had relented after she'd told them she wanted no one else. They acquiesced and as a young girl of seventeen she'd married Jeremy.

Now at twenty-three, she was a widow in black.

Jeremy's family had finally left as the night drew in. Dinner was quiet in the formal dining room; the staff brought her favourite—a solid and warming meal. The staff, even now, stood with her, protecting her as did her own family. Now, settled around the large fire in the parlour, she would tell them everything.

Isabelle and Elspeth crowded in beside her. Warming her more effectively than the fire could, while their husbands, Aeddan and Langdon, filled the wing chairs. They were strong, reliable men, and the right partners for her sisters, Louisa knew.

"What do you wish to tell us, dearest?" Elspeth gripped her hands.

"He… Jeremy. The night of the accident? He'd been out. There was a tremendous storm which blew in and he ventured home in it. But he'd… He had a mistress, Elspeth. A woman in the neighbouring township. He'd been with her."

Silence descended on the room. "You're sure?" Aeddan leaned forward, imbuing the question with power.

"Yes. I received a note yesterday. Before your arrival." She fished about in the pocket of her gown and drew it out with shaking hands. "Here, read it for yourself."

She didn't wish to ever see it again. The memory imprinted on her mind.

Dear Mrs Lavenwood,

Allow me to offer my condolences. Dearest Jeremy and I were as close as any man and woman could be. He confided in me, prior to the accident, that your recent interesting state and the doting on your daughter were difficult for him. He was a man who needed to be first in everything, including your affections, especially given his unfortunate position at birth.

However, it is my expectation that a token of his regard will be forthcoming to me. My expenses do not end with Jeremy's death as there is a child. As such, I feel it is only right, in light of the closeness we shared, that I should be granted a portion of his fortune, which I understand he personally used to purchase your family home.

I will, of course, be more than willing to engage with your solicitor at a time that is convenient to him.

Lady Pamela Jezerey

Aeddan swore and thrust the paper to Langdon, whose eyes glittered with fury as he read the missive. The paper then was read by both Elspeth and Isabelle.

"He had no claim on the house?" Aeddan queried. "So, he cannot gain any control of the Forster Shipping money or property?"

Elspeth shook her head. "When we drew up the marriage settlement, both Isabelle and I ensured the house did not pass from the family's control, nor any of the business. Louisa was young, and it was the best way we could protect her. The portion that went to Louisa was significant, but was not used in any way for the upkeep of the house or to pay the staff. They were all in the employ of Forster Shipping."

Langdon smiled. "And of course, he duly signed that?"

"Oh yes," Isabelle said with a smile. "We had our man of business bring in a senior solicitor from London to ensure everything was watertight. We love our sister." She shrugged then turned to Louisa. "We wanted to ensure her needs and those of any children were protected."

Aeddan stood and stalked to the fireplace, looked at it for a long moment. "With regards to this child this woman is claiming is your husband's. Has anyone questioned the veracity of her claim? That the child…"

Langdon nodded. "Yes, I agree. We need to establish if indeed the child was Jeremy's."

"No. I don't wish you to do that. Not openly or behind my back." Too many things had occurred, things Louisa knew nothing about until now, and she'd not allow anyone to hide this kind of information from her. Never again.

"But dearest," Elspeth stated, but stilled as Louisa shook her head.

"But you should know, Louisa. If the child *is* his… His parents should take some kind of steps."

Her laugh was discordant. "No, they won't. If this child is his, it's a bastard…" She huffed, because she knew that sounded callous. "I don't know the right answer, but if I've learned anything during this time, it's that his family shies away from truths that do not conform with their norm. Now then, I need to make decisions. Good decisions."

"But the child…" Isabelle leaned in. "It's innocent. It should be protected."

Louisa shook her head. "If there's a child, and I don't know the answer, what if it's not his?"

"Then we find out," answered Langdon. "Once the truth is known, then you can make a decision."

Louisa bit her lip, hearing for the first time the truth in his words. "Find out then," she whispered. "If it's not…"

"You have no responsibility," answered Isabelle.

"Perhaps now is the time to travel up to our properties," Elspeth added. "Take some time away while this is—"

Louisa inhaled deeply, felt the air in her chest, and prepared herself mentally. "Elspeth, much as I would love to run away from all this, you've both sheltered me for far too long. It's time I stood on my own. Took control of my life. I intend to see this through and to become an equal shareholder in Forster Shipping. I have two daughters who need to see their mama as an independent woman, and for too long, I allowed others to direct my life and felt secure in the lack of knowledge. If I've learned nothing else, it's that I'm strong and capable."

Louisa sat upright in the chair and stared forward at first one then the other sister.

When they both opened their mouths to remonstrate, Louisa held up a hand. "No. It's true. I will no longer be passive, sisters. I will see this mess of Jeremy's through, and as for Jezerey, well, whatever you learn will be dealt with by the solicitors. There is a full year of black, then when I can wear other colours. This is the time when I will consider my options."

This new Louisa was merely the tip as plans and ideas were unveiling in her mind. Not yet fully formed, but beginning to cascade. *I need time.* Time to let go of the dream, time to formulate her plan, and time to unravel the threads of a life barely lived before she could decide what and who the new Louisa would be.

"Living here? It's no longer enough, and I will need your support soon. Lady Constance is most insistent I should move to the Hall…" Before her sisters could speak, Louisa held up a hand. "…which I have no intentions of doing. She plans to take control of me and my life and my daughters' lives too. That I will not tolerate. Just as I will not tolerate her waspish friends and their whispers."

"We'll put paid to the biddies, my love," Elspeth answered. "You'll have our unwavering support and those of our circle. All you need to do is ask."

"Good," she said. "Because I've already sent for our man of business and the solicitor from London. I will stand on my own two feet, and I will protect what is mine and ours."

Available from Love Books Publishing
https://books2read.com/MerryWidow

Direct Autographed Copy
https://imogenenix.net/product/a-very-merry-widow/

ALSO BY IMOGENE NIX

<u>Warriors of the Elector</u>

- Star of Ishtar
- Starline
- Starfire
- Star of the Fleet
- Starburst
- The Star of Eternity

The Star of Ishtar & Starline - Print

Starfire & Star of the Fleet - Print

Starburst & The Star of Eternity - Print

<u>Blood Secrets</u>

- The Blood Bride
- The Illuminated Witch
- The Sorcerer's Touch

<u>*The Secrets World:*</u>

<u>Blood Secrets</u>

- The Blood Bride
- The Illuminated Witch
- The Sorcerer's Touch

<u>House Secrets</u>

- As Dawn Breaks
- Immortal Consequences
- Edge of Night

All That Glitters - a House Secrets Novella

Danu's Secrets

* The Downfall of Padraic O'Shaunessy
* A Demon Called Grace
* The Secrets of Danu

The Automaton Series

* Haven House
* Nobel Crest

The Search Duology

* Miss Elspeth's Desire
* Miss Isabelle's Craving

Duology World Novels

* A Very Merry Widow

Reunion Trilogy

* War's End
* The Assassin
* Executing Justice

The Reunion Trilogy in Paperback

Sex Love & Aliens

* Tangled Webs
* False Webs
* Covert Webs

<u>21st Testing Protocol</u>

- Cyborg: Redux
- Children Of A Greater Evil
- When Evil Came To Stay
- Finis: The War To End All Wars

<u>Celtic Cupid Trilogy</u>

- Blame The Wine
- A Stranger's Embrace
- Revenge On Cupid

The Celtic Cupid Trilogy in Paperback

<u>Zombieology</u>

- The Reset
- I Dream of Zombies
- The Six Million Dollar Zombie
- Make Room For Zombies
- Days of Our Zombies
- Unnamed Zobiology title

<u>Out Of Time Series</u>

- Flight In time (coming in 2025)
- Bound In Time (coming in 2026)
- Running Out of Time (coming in 2026)

<u>Knights of Pleasure</u>

- Silken Knights

<u>Single Titles</u>

The Chocolate Affair (also in Print)

Falling In Love Again (Previously A Sapphire For Karina)

BioCybe (also in Print)

Hesparia's Tears (also in Print)

Tomorrow's Promise (also in Print)

A Bar In Paris (also in Print)

Inheritance Of The Blood (also in Print)

The Plan (also in Print)

Loving Memories (also in Print)

Hero of Heartbreak Hill (also in Print)

My One & Only (also in Print)

Curse Bound (also in Print)

<u>Non Fiction</u>

Self Publishing: Absolute Beginners Guide (With Suzi Love)

<u>Written as Ciara Cave</u>

25 Curated Ways To Get Rid Of Telemarketers

Book Signings for Absolute Beginners

ABOUT THE AUTHOR

Imogene is published in a range of romance genres including Paranormal, Science Fiction and Contemporary. She is mainly published in the UK and USA.

In 2010, Imogene Nix (the pen name not Imogene herself) was born. Imogene sat down and worked tirelessly for 3 months culminating in the book Starline, which became the first in a trilogy titled, "Warriors of the Elector." Since then she's had over 30 titles published and is now focusing on hybridising herself - with a mixture of traditionally published and self-published works.

In fact, she's taking control of many of her back catalogue books, which are slowly re-releasing as self-published titles.

Imogene is a member of a range of professional organisations world wide, and believes in the mantra of mentoring and paying it forward and is actively involved in mentorship (through NaNoWrimo and her vlog: In The Chair With Imogene Nix) and tutoring of new and upcoming authors.

In her spare time she loves to drink coffee, wine & eat chocolate and is parenting her spoiled dog and a ferocious cat along with her husband and daughter and looks forward to weekends away with her husband in their caravan "The Seven Year Hitch!" Do look forward to her caravan romance at some point!

Lastly, Imogene returned to University during the pandemic and in 2023 completed her Master of Communication and now is enrolled in her PhD… She's a glutton for punishment, but never fear, imogene continues to write and publish books for readers to enjoy!

To Contact Imogene
www.imogenenix.net
imogene@imogenenix.net

Sign up for her newsletter at
https://www.imogenenix.net/Signup

facebook.com/ImogeneNix
x.com/ImogeneNix
instagram.com/ImogeneNix
bookbub.com/authors/imogenenix